AF586071

Evincepub
Publishing

Published by

# Evincepub Publishing

Shivam Complex, Bilaspur, Chhattisgarh 495009
Ph.: +91-9171810321
e-Mail: publish@evincepub.com
Website: www.evincepub.com



**First Edition: 2024**

ISBN: 978-93-5673-700-6

Publication Month:


This book is also available on;
Amazon, Flipkart, Evincepub.com

# Kashmiran

**Soudia Parveen**

# ABOUT THE BOOK

I welcome you to step into the mind-bending world of my novel "Kashmiran," that takes you on an emotional rollercoaster with its main character, Reeda. Follow Reeda's journey as she encounters different men, leading to a heartbreak that shakes her world. Seeking a fresh start, she decides to pursue higher studies in a new place. But the story doesn't stop there.

This novel peels back the layers of Reeda's mind, exploring her inner struggles and strengths as she tries to heal. The narrative gets into the depth of psychological twists and turns of her thoughts, creating an immersive experience that blurs the line between reality and her internal world.

Just when you think you have it figured out, "Kashmiran" delivers a surprising finale that will leave you questioning everything.

# ABOUT THE AUTHOR

Soudia Parveen, hailing from West Bengal, is not just an author but a literary dynamo whose writing is as essential to her existence as breathing. Her journey into the world of publishing faced challenges until a perceptive literary agent recognized her potential in 2020, marking the beginning of a professional literary life. Known for her notable works like 'World of My Words,' 'Alfazon Ki Tijori,' and 'The Enclosed Confession,' Soudia has carved a niche for herself as a versatile author, book reviewer, podcaster, and interviewer. Currently practicing as a clinical psychologist and life coach, she enriches her narratives by exploring diverse themes. Active contributions to The Rise Insight, The Asian Literature Newspaper, and various magazines showcase her commitment to storytelling. Soudia Parveen's literary odyssey is a celebration of passion, purpose, and a deep dive into the complexities of the human experience.

# ACKNOWLEDGEMENT

I am sincerely thankful to the incredible readers who have been constantly supporting, not just for 'Kashmiran,' but for my previous works as well.

A special shoutout to my parents, Mr Sk Ishaque Ali and Mrs Hena Khatun, for giving me the space to think and write. And big love to my sister, Sheerat Fatema, for being the first to hear my story and pushing me to put it out there.

A tip of the hat to Mr Vikram Singh Thakur, my publisher and friend, for crafting a standout cover that truly fits best with the title 'Kashmiran', giving the book a distinct identity.

I am equally grateful to Ms Arpita for taking the time to read my novel and share her thoughts – your insights have added depth to the story.

Last but not the least, a huge thanks to my buddy Mr Abraar Rashid Reshi. His support to educate me about Kashmiri culture have been like the secret sauce that makes 'Kashmiran' what it is. He's been my go-to guide, teaching me the ins and outs of Kashmiri culture, language, and all the reasons you can't help but fall for the place. For the past two years, he's been my constant source, sharing every bit of info about Kashmir's heritage. Without him, this book wouldn't have the same flavor. Thanks a bunch!

Kudos to everyone who played a role, big or small, in making 'Kashmiran' a reality, I'm grateful beyond words.

Regards,

Soudia Parveen

# CONTENTS

Prior to embarking on this novel, I'd like to offer explanations for certain phrases I have used in this novel which are in Arabic, Urdu, and Koshur to enrich the reader's understanding.

**List of phrases with their meanings: -**

1. **MUSLIMAH: -** "Muslimah" is an Arabic term used to refer to a Muslim woman. It is derived from the word "Muslim," which means a follower of Islam, and the suffix "-ah," which is often added to denote the female gender. So, "Muslimah" specifically signifies a female adherent of Islam.
2. **KHALA**: - "Khala" is an Urdu and Arabic term that translates to "maternal aunt" in English. It is used to refer to the sister of one's mother.
3. **SUNNAH**: - "Sunnah" refers to the practices, actions, sayings, and approvals of Prophet Muhammad (peace be upon him) in Islam. It serves as a significant source of guidance for Muslims, complementing the teachings of the Quran. Following the Sunnah is considered a way for Muslims to emulate the Prophet's exemplary life and behaviour.
4. **SUNNI MUSLIM**: - A Sunni Muslim is an adherent of Sunni Islam, which is the largest branch of Islam. Sunnis follow the Sunnah (traditions) of the Prophet Muhammad, as well as the teachings of the Quran.

5. **BISMILLAH: -** "Bismillah" is an Arabic phrase that translates to "In the name of Allah" in English. It is an invocation that Muslims often recite before starting various activities, meals, or any significant undertaking. It reflects a recognition of Allah's name and seeking His blessings and guidance.
6. **ASTAGFIRULLAH: -** "Astagfirullah" is an Arabic phrase commonly used by Muslims, and it translates to "I seek forgiveness from Allah" in English. It is an expression of repentance and seeking pardon for any wrongdoing or sins. Muslims often use this phrase as a way to seek Allah's mercy and forgiveness.
7. **SUBHAN'ALLAH: -** "Subhan'Allah" is an Arabic phrase that translates to "Glory be to Allah" or "Exalted is Allah" in English. It is an expression of praise and acknowledgment of the perfection and greatness of Allah. Muslims use this phrase to glorify and recognize the absolute beauty and flawlessness of Allah's attributes.
8. **ALHAMDULILLAH**: - "Alhamdulillah" is an Arabic phrase that translates to "All praise is due to Allah" in English. It is an expression of gratitude and thankfulness to Allah for His blessings, guidance, and all that is good. Muslims commonly use this phrase to acknowledge and appreciate the mercy and bounty of Allah in various aspects of life.

9. **ASSALAMU-ALAIKUM:** - "Assalamu-Alaikum" is an Arabic greeting that translates to "Peace be upon you" in English. It is a common and traditional greeting among Muslims.
10. **WALAIKUM ASLAM**: - The response to "Assalamu-Alaikum" is "Wa-Alaikum Assalam," which means "And upon you be at peace." This exchange reflects a wish for peace and blessings upon the one being greeted.
11. **ALIMAH: -** "Alimah" is an Arabic term that refers to a knowledgeable or learned woman, particularly in the context of Islamic scholarship. An Alimah is a female scholar who has studied and gained expertise in Islamic knowledge, including the Quran, Hadith (sayings and actions of Prophet Muhammad), and other Islamic sciences. She is recognized for her understanding of religious matters and may play a role in teaching and guiding others in matters of faith and practice.
12. **KEHWA: -** "Kehwa" refers to a traditional green tea preparation that is popular in Kashmir and some other regions. It is often flavoured with spices such as cardamom, cinnamon, and cloves, and sometimes includes almonds or saffron. Kehwa is known for its aromatic and refreshing qualities and is often served in social gatherings or during special occasions.

13. **WAZWAN**: - "Wazwan" is a traditional multi-course feast in Kashmiri cuisine, often associated with special occasions and celebrations. It consists of a variety of dishes, typically prepared with rich and aromatic flavours. Wazwan is known for its elaborate preparation and presentation, and it includes dishes like various types of kebabs, curries, and rice preparations. It holds cultural significance and is a symbol of hospitality and communal celebration in the Kashmiri tradition.
14. **JAZAK ALLAH**: - "Jazak Allah" is an Arabic expression that translates to "May Allah reward you" or "May Allah recompense you" in English. It is often used to express gratitude or to acknowledge someone's kindness, help, or good deeds. Muslims use this phrase to convey appreciation and to pray for Allah's blessings upon the person who has done something positive or beneficial.
15. **ALISHAAN: -** "Alishan" is a Persian and Urdu term that translates to "lofty" or "majestic" in English. It is often used to describe something grand, impressive, or elevated in stature. The term can be applied to various contexts, such as describing a majestic landscape, an imposing building, or a person's elevated character.
16. **YA RABB: -** "Ya Rabb" is an Arabic phrase that translates to "O Lord" or "O God" in

English. It is an invocation used by Muslims to address and call upon Allah, expressing supplication, dependence, and a sense of submission. The term "Ya Rabb" is often employed in prayers and moments of seeking guidance, mercy, or assistance from the Almighty.

17. **YA ALLAH REHAM**: - "Ya Allah, reham" is an Arabic and Urdu phrase that translates to "O Allah, have mercy" in English. It is a supplication or prayer expressing a plea for Allah's compassion, kindness, and mercy. This phrase is often used by individuals seeking Allah's benevolence and forgiveness in times of difficulty or when asking for divine assistance.
18. **ALLAH HAFIZ: -** "Allah Hafiz" is an Arabic phrase commonly used in Urdu and other languages, and it translates to "May Allah protect you" or "May Allah keep you safe" in English. It is a parting phrase used when saying goodbye, wishing someone well, and invoking Allah's protection upon them as they depart.
19. **SHABBA KHAIR: -** "Shabba Khair" (شبّ بخير) is an Urdu and Arabic phrase that translates to "Good night" in English. It is commonly used to bid someone farewell or wish them a good night before they go to sleep.
20. **INNA LILLAHI WA INNA ILAYHI RAJI'UN: -** "Inna lillahi wa inna ilayhi raji'un" (إِنَّا لِلَّهِ وَإِنَّا إِلَيْهِ رَاجِعونَ) is an Arabic phrase that

translates to "Surely we belong to Allah and to Him shall we return" in English. This expression is often recited by Muslims in times of grief, sorrow, or upon hearing news of someone's death. It reflects the acknowledgment of life's transient nature and the belief that ultimately all individuals belong to Allah and will return to Him.

Thank you so much for choosing my novel to read. I hope these few phrases with their meanings will be useful while reading the entire novel since it's mostly based on Kashmir and kashmiri lifestyle and linguistics.

**– Soudia Parveen**

"WANDE TZALE,
SHEEN GALI
BEYI YI BAHAAR"

WINTER WILL FLEE,
SNOW WILL MELT,
AGAIN SPRING WILL MAKE IT'S PRESENCE FELT.
~QALAAM-E-MAHJOOR

IMAGE CREDITS: ©ABRARRESHI

# IMPORTANT NOTE TO READERS

This story is entirely made up, meaning it's not real. A chapter talks about a character named Bilal who gets caught up in a secret mission in Kashmir. While it explores themes of spying and betrayal, it's important to know that none of it actually happened. Still, if these kinds of topics might bother you, it's a good idea to be careful while reading.

# PROLOGUE

As I sit here, pen in hand, reminiscing about that fateful day on the Dal Lake, a whirlwind of emotions floods my heart. My name is Reeda, and this is the story of how a simple outing with Bilal, my neighbour and soon-to-be husband, changed the course of my life forever. In a world where arranged marriages are the norm, I never expected to find love and understanding in such an unconventional way. Join me as I recount the events of that extraordinary day, filled with interesting incidents, serious conversations, and unexpected revelations.

The sun was rising, making the Dal Lake look golden and peaceful. The air was fresh, smelling like flowers, and the leaves were gently rustling. When I got on the wooden boat, I felt excited and a bit nervous. Bilal, wearing traditional Kashmiri clothes, greeted me with a friendly smile that made me feel comfortable.

Bilal: "Reeda, I'm so glad you agreed to come on this outing with me. I've always admired your spirit and wanted to get to know you better."

Reeda: "Thank you, Bilal. I must admit, I was hesitant at first, but something about your genuine nature compelled me to give this a chance."

As the boat glided across the serene waters, we found ourselves immersed in the breathtaking beauty of the surroundings. The majestic mountains stood tall, their peaks adorned with a dusting of snow, while beautifully crafted shikaras floated gracefully nearby. The silence between us was comfortable, allowing us to appreciate the peacefulness of the moment.

Reeda: "Bilal, I never imagined that our first meeting outside of our families' presence would be in such a scenic setting. It feels like a dream."

Bilal: "Indeed, Reeda. Sometimes, life surprises us in the most unexpected ways. I wanted to take this opportunity to get to know you beyond the boundaries of our arranged marriage. I believe that understanding and friendship are the foundations of a successful relationship."

Reeda: "You speak with wisdom, Bilal. I too believe that a marriage should be built on trust, respect, and shared values. It's refreshing to hear your perspective."

As the boat floated further into the lake, an interesting incident unfolded before our eyes. A flock of colourful birds took flight, their wings creating a mesmerising dance in the sky. We watched in awe, our eyes locked on the graceful spectacle.

Reeda: "Look, Bilal! Isn't it fascinating how these birds move in perfect harmony? It's as if they understand each other without uttering a single word."

Bilal: "Indeed, Reeda. Nature has a way of teaching us valuable lessons. Just like those birds, I believe that a strong bond between two individuals can be formed through understanding and communication."

Reeda: "You're right, Bilal. It's essential for us to have open and honest conversations about our expectations, dreams, and aspirations. Only then can we truly undertake this journey together."

As the day progressed, our conversations grew deeper and more meaningful. We discussed our families, our dreams, and our fears. We shared stories of our childhood, our favourite books, and our aspirations for the future. It was during these serious conversations that I realised Bilal was not just a neighbour or a prospective husband, but a kindred spirit who understood and respected me.

In the midst of our heartfelt discussions, the sun began its descent, setting a warm glow over the lake. The boat slowly made its way back to the shore, but our connection had already set sail on a new course. As the sun dipped below the horizon, Bilal leaned in and gently kissed me. Little did I know that this one day date on the Dal Lake would mark the beginning of a beautiful love story, one that would defy societal norms and expectations.

To be continued……

## 18 YEARS AGO

*In a cosy and inviting therapy room, Dr. Khan sits across from Reeda, who is visibly distressed. The room is filled with a gentle ambiance, and Dr. Khan speaks in a reassuring tone.*

Dr. Khan: Reeda, I know things have been really hard for you lately. It's okay to feel the way you do. I'm here to help and support you.

Reeda looks at Dr. Khan, her eyes reflecting a mix of pain and confusion.

Dr. Khan: Now, Reeda, I want you to promise me something. Promise that you'll always take good care of yourself, no matter what happens.

Reeda: nods slowly

Dr. Khan: Good. You're strong, and you can get through tough times. But if ever you feel really, really sad or upset, promise me you'll talk to someone you trust—a friend, a family member, or even a teacher.

Reeda: softly whispers I will.

Dr. Khan: That's my brave girl. And there's something else we need to talk about. Sometimes, things might happen that remind you of the difficult times.

These things are called triggers. They can make you feel scared or sad, even if the bad things are over.

Reeda: looks curious

Dr. Khan: For you, a trigger might be something like hearing unkind words or feeling left out. It's important to recognize these triggers so that you can protect yourself. If you ever feel like a trigger is making you too upset, it's okay to take a break and let someone know how you're feeling.

Reeda: nods

Dr. Khan: Also, Reeda, I want you to promise me something else. If ever you find that these sad feelings don't go away or if they get too big to handle, it might be helpful to talk to a special helper called a therapist. They're like friends who are really good at helping people feel better on the inside.

Reeda: (whispers) Okay.

Dr. Khan: You're not alone in this, Reeda. Taking care of your feelings is important, and it's okay to ask for help. Promise me you'll do that.

Reeda: (softly) I promise.

Dr. Khan: That's my brave girl. Remember, you have the strength to face whatever comes your way. I believe in you.

Dr. Khan continues to support Reeda throughout their sessions, providing guidance and encouragement as she works towards healing.

-

*On the last day of Reeda's counselling sessions, Dr. Khan sat down with Mr. and Mrs. Reshi to talk about some important things for the future. The therapy room felt calm and comforting, marking the end of Reeda's journey through healing from the tough times at school.*

*In this final session, Dr. Khan shared practical advice and safety measures with Reeda's parents, emphasizing the need for a nurturing environment to continue supporting Reeda's emotional well-being.*

***Flashback Scene: -***

*Dr. Khan, sitting across from Mr. and Mrs. Reshi in the consultation room, expresses concern about Reeda's recent struggles.*

Dr. Khan: Mr. and Mrs. Reshi, I understand that Reeda has faced significant challenges at school, and her emotional well-being has been deeply affected. It's crucial for us to work together to support her during this difficult time.

Mr. Reshi: We're really worried about her, Doctor. She hasn't spoken a word since that incident at school.

Dr. Khan: I empathize with Reeda's situation, and it's clear that she's going through a difficult time. I want you both to be aware of potential triggers that might further impact her emotional state. Reeda is particularly vulnerable to experiences that remind her of the bullying incident.

Mrs. Reshi: What should we watch out for, Doctor?

Dr. Khan: Firstly, any form of verbal or physical aggression can be a severe trigger for Reeda. Given her past experiences, it's essential to create a safe environment at home. Additionally, be cautious about exposing her to situations that might mimic the conditions she faced during the bullying incident.

Mr. Reshi: We'll do our best to protect her.

Dr. Khan: Excellent. Also, keep an eye on her social interactions. If she begins to withdraw or show signs of distress in certain social situations, it could be indicative of underlying trauma. Encourage open communication with Reeda, and if you notice any changes in her behavior or mood, consider seeking professional help promptly.

Mrs. Reshi: We'll make sure to pay close attention to her emotional well-being.

Dr. Khan: Lastly, I recommend considering therapy for Reeda in the future. A trained therapist can help her navigate these difficult emotions and work towards healing. If her mute state persists or if you observe any signs of depression, anxiety, or post-traumatic stress, seeking professional help becomes even more critical.

Mr. Reshi: Thank you, Doctor. We'll be alert and do everything we can for Reeda.

*Dr. Khan provides Mr. and Mrs. Reshi with resources for local therapists and support groups, emphasizing the importance of ongoing care and communication within the family.*

# THE RESHI FAMILY

# 1

Reeda, a devout *'Muslimah'* hailing from the picturesque city of Srinagar, belonged to a 'Sunni' Muslim family. Reeda's family was like a big storybook, and Kashmir was the setting for all their adventures. Living in Srinagar, they weren't just locals; they were part of the living history of the place.

The family gatherings were like treasure troves of stories, with the older folks passing down tales and traditions. Festivals weren't just celebrations; they were a way of keeping the unique Kashmiri culture alive and kicking. Reeda was the most admired and blessed child in the entire family. Being the only girl in the crew, she was treated like the princess of her family.

Reeda's parents, Mr. and Mrs. Reshi, were like the superheroes of their home. Her dad, Mr. Rashid Reshi, worked in an office, making sure everything was okay. But the real magic happened at home with her mom, Mrs. Razia Reshi.

Reeda's father, Mr. Rashid Reshi, had a job that was kind of like being a guardian for the government. Every day, he would head off to his office, making sure things were running smoothly. Even though he had this serious job, when it came to Reeda, his only daughter, he was like a teddy bear – all soft and loving.

Despite the demands of his job, Mr. Reshi made sure to find time for Reeda. He'd listen to her dreams, help with homework, and sometimes, they'd even sneak in a little adventure together. Whether it was a weekend outing or just sharing stories over dinner, he cherished every moment with Reeda.

When Reeda decided to dive into English studies, Mr. Reshi couldn't have been prouder. He might not have known all the fancy terms, but he understood that his daughter had found something she loved. In his eyes, Reeda wasn't just a student; she was a bright star, and he was her biggest fan.

Their home became a blend of seriousness and laughter, with Mr. Reshi's love for his only daughter shining through. His job was more than just paperwork and meetings; it was about creating a safe space for Reeda to dream big. In the end, it wasn't just a job for Mr. Reshi; it was a way to support the dreams of the one he loved the most – his beloved daughter, Reeda.

To the contrary, Reeda's mother had a different kind of job. She was like the captain of their home, steering the ship and making sure everything was cosy and full of love. Even though people might call it being a housewife, Mrs. Reshi saw it as being the heart of the family.

Mrs. Reshi was more than just a homemaker; she turned their place into a comfy, happy zone. When Reeda said she loves reading books and writing, her mom got super excited. She created this cool reading corner at home, filled with books. It was like a little nest where Reeda could dive into her love for literature.

Beyond the walls of her home, Reeda's passion bloomed in the world of writing. With a keen interest in her roots, she dedicated her blog to the highs and lows of Kashmir. Her words not only captured the political turbulence but also delved into the heart of the region's soul.

Yet, Reeda's writing went beyond the political canvas. She painted poetic pictures that celebrated the beauty of the mountains and the serenity of her surroundings. Her verses became a tribute to the majestic landscapes that cradled her hometown, showcasing the grace of the mountains and the tales they whispered in the wind. Her blog wasn't just a diary of the place; it seemed like a love letter to the stunning mountains that guard her hometown.

In a world that sometimes felt vast and lonely, Reeda found solace in her words. Each blog post and every poem became a reflection of her connection to both her faith and the breathtaking homeland she called her own.

As the youngest and only daughter, she is surrounded by the love and protective watch of her four elder brothers.

In the heart of Srinagar, Reeda's family was an adventurous tale with the threads of four elder brothers — Rahi, Abrar, Razaq, and Umer. Each brother, like a character in a story, played a distinct role in the intricate narrative of their family and, in some ways, the broader canvas of Kashmir.

Rahi, the eldest, stood tall as a former army man who had transitioned into an undercover agent. His days were shrouded in secrecy, a silent guardian veiled in the intricate realm of intelligence gathering that significantly impacts the security dynamics of Kashmir.

Rahi's service went beyond the confines of their home, reaching into the very pulse of Kashmir's security and the delicate balance that defined the region.

Unlike Rahi, who worked in secret missions, Abrar's thing was totally different. He is into real estate – you know, building cool stuff. It isn't just about bricks and walls; he is like a storyteller using concrete. Each building he created had a tale, and these stories were changing the way Srinagar looked.

Abrar, the real estate 'guru', has a secret side hustle – he fancied himself a stock market whiz. It's like he's got this financial superhero cape that he puts on after sundown. Some days, he's riding the stock market wave like a pro surfer, shouting, "Masha'Allah, Allah'hu'Akbar!" And on other days, he's scratching his head, wondering how the numbers played a prank on him.

Abrar, the daytime builder of dreams, transforms into a nighttime financial wizard. It's a bit like a comedy show where he's juggling numbers and doing this money dance that keeps everyone guessing. In the novel of Abrar's life, each stock market escapade is a page-turner, filled with suspense, laughs, and a touch of financial drama.

Last but not the least, Razaq and Umer, the software developers, found their niche in the digital realm. Their fingers danced on keyboards, crafting lines of code that transcended physical boundaries. In a world increasingly connected by technology, their work wasn't just about programming; it was about weaving the digital fabric that linked Kashmir to the global landscape.

To conclude, Reeda was on a never ending adventurous life with her four brothers which included Rahi with his secret missions, Abrar crafting modern fairytales, and Razaq and Umer working their digital magic. Together, these brothers are like the superheroes of Kashmir, each adding their unique flavour to the big adventure story of their homeland.

As each family member pursued their own paths, they carried a piece of Kashmir with them. Whether Rahi embarked on secret missions, Abrar crafted modern tales in real estate, or Reeda penned her poetic reflections, every sibling added a distinct chapter to the ongoing story of their family and its deep ties to the captivating land of Kashmir.

# KASHMIRAN

# 2

Born and raised in the enchanting valleys of Kashmir, she carried the essence of the region in every step.

Growing up surrounded by the majestic mountains, pristine lakes, and the vibrant culture of Srinagar, Reeda's connection to Kashmir was more than just geographical. Her love for her homeland wasn't just about the breathtaking landscapes; it was about the traditions, the warmth of the people, and the rich mixture of Kashmiri art and literature.

One day, Reeda sat by the window of her family home in Srinagar. Inspired by the gentle breeze carrying the sweet fragrance of saffron-infused tea and the hidden tales whispered by the valleys, she decided to share her love for Kashmir through the art of words. That day marked the beginning of a journey that would earn her a unique title.

As she poured her heart into blogs that spoke of the verdant meadows, the snow-capped mountains, and the colourful culture of Kashmir, Reeda became a storyteller with a digital pen. Her words produced positive feelings within readers across borders, capturing not just the pleasing mountains but the soul of a region steeped in tradition.

Her blogs unfolded tales of Kehwa, the soul-soothing elixir that adorned her family's breakfast rituals. She mentioned that with each sip, she felt the warmth of conversations where her grandparents would share stories of the ancient spice trade that infused Kehwa with more than just flavours – it carried the history of Kashmir's aromatic past. In other blogs she would mention that as the snowflakes danced in Gulmarg, she wrapped herself in a Pashmina shawl that bore the stories of artisans crafting dreams. Her blogs narrated the artistry behind each delicate weave, a story of generations passing down the craft. The Pashmina became a wearable poem, embroidered with echoes of her adventures in Sonmarg's meadows and the tranquil moments spent by Dal Lake.

Dal Lake wasn't just a scenic setting in Reeda's life; it was a stage for personal stories. In her blogs, she recounted the day she floated lanterns on the shimmering waters during a family celebration. Dal Lake became a canvas where memories, like the reflections of Chinars, painted an ever-evolving masterpiece.

Reeda's life had a silent companion – the Clock Tower. Her blogs took readers through the time she and her friends gathered under its arches, savoring hot snacks from a street vendor. The ticking hands became witnesses to friendships, laughter, and the timeless moments when the city seemed to pause, acknowledging the beauty of fleeting instants.

In Reeda's blogs, these elements weren't mere topics but a story where she invited her readers to step into Kashmir's unending miracles, where every sip, every weave, every ripple, and every thread carried the spice of a unique journey.

Through her poems and writings, she painted pictures of the valleys, narrated tales of resilience, and celebrated the unique blend of tradition and modernity that defined Kashmir which made her readers call her by the term 'Kashmiran' which wasn't just a casual label but given because she was recognized as a woman whose veins flowed not just blood but the very spirit of Kashmir.

# THIS SIDE, RAHI!

# 3

I am Rahi, the eldest among us, and my life has taken me through the twists and turns of covert operations.

Beyond the façade of an ex-armyman turned undercover agent, I found purpose in being the unspoken bodyguard to my youngest sister, Reeda.

I stand not just as a brother but as the silent custodian of Reeda's well-being.

Reeda, driven by her deep love for literature and poetry, chose to pursue English Honours, a path that mirrored her passion.

In the academic realm, Reeda's dedication and enthusiasm began to shine. Her early academic years might have been considered average, but as she stepped into the corridors of Kashmir University, something ignited within her. The subjects that once posed challenges became her forte, earning her a series of certificates of excellence. Each certificate was like a badge of honour for her.

As Reeda progressed through her Bachelor's degree, her commitment and hard work caught the attention of both professors and peers. The recognition extended beyond the confines of her grades, landing her among the ten best students. It was a remarkable feat that spoke volumes about her dedication to her studies and her ability to excel in the world of literature.

Yet, Reeda's academic journey was not just about certificates or rankings but a story full of resilience and growth.

Her radiant spirit, the sparkle in her eyes as she immersed herself in the world of literature, had been a source of pride but I hate William Shakespeare.

Anyways, I didn't even know the spelling of literature until my boards.

I remember a particular incident during Reeda's school days when she received a vintage styled love letter. The mischievous glint in her eyes couldn't escape my notice. Though I maintained the stoic appearance, deep down, I couldn't help but chuckle at the innocence of it all. Yet, as her self-appointed guardian, I took it upon myself to discreetly investigate the sender.

The unsuspecting boy found himself face-to-face with a stern Rahi, a figure he had likely never expected to encounter. I, the silent protector, delivered a command without hitting the boy. I still remembered how he was shivering after knowing my relationship with Reeda.

I had a straight face while delivering him these words: "If I catch you sending these useless love letters and distracting my only sister from her academics, I won't hesitate to push you into the chilling waters of Jhelum in winters or even crack your neck if necessary."

He never saw my sister's face after that. It worked, but my sister adopted a tough attitude towards me from then on.

'Why did you bother him?' she firmly asked while sipping kehwa. 'Bother whom? Rahmat chacha? For bringing figs?' I retorted, as if I didn't know what was going on.

'Oh, come on! Enough of your bodyguard mode. Please stop bothering me and my friends. This is not the way you react to a person who is my friend,' she desperately banged on the table while delivering this dialogue.

'Hello, Kashmiran, do not forget you belong to an Islamic family. Fear Allah in regards to this. Isn't he a non-mahram? Don't you know the preachings of our Prophet (pbuh)? Haven't you read the Qur'an? Do you not know that interactions between non-mahrams are forbidden in Islam because they may give rise to unlawful emotions that inevitably lead to illegitimate relationships between a man and a woman?' I furiously questioned her all at once.

She went mute. The entire family was staring at me out of curiosity, as if I were going to start reciting the entire Qur'an then.

A few years passed, and observing my sister's tough attitude, I pondered over ways to guide her back towards the path of Islamic teachings. That's when I decided to send her to our neighbour's place to learn more about the deen (the religion or belief of a Muslim).

Romana 'khala', known for her deep knowledge and devotion, became the chosen mentor for this venture. Romana 'khala', a widow with a heart as vast as the valleys surrounding our neighbourhood, is a jar full of patience and kindness. She resides in a quaint home adorned with the fragrance of incense and the echoes of Quranic verses. Her only son, Bilal, three years older than Reeda, is a finance analyst with a penchant for balancing numbers and a heart generous enough to inherit the warmth of his mother.

Romana 'khala', with her serene countenance and gentle personality, became a maternal figure not only for her son but for the entire neighbourhood. Widowed at a young age, she faced life's challenges with grace and resilience, turning her home into a sanctuary of solace for those in need.

Bilal, Romana Khala's son, inherited not just his mother's financial acumen but also her compassionate spirit. Despite the demands of his career, he never let the responsibilities of the material world overshadow his commitment to family and community.

This is where I knew I was sending my sister in good hands.

One evening, as the golden hues of the setting sun bathed our neighbourhood, Reeda reluctantly agreed to attend classes with Romana Khala. The first session was met with a mix of curiosity and apprehension.

During one particular class, Romana Khala shared a story that left a profound impact on Reeda. It was the tale of Aisha (RA), the wife of Prophet Muhammad (PBUH), known for her wisdom and scholarly contributions. As Romana Khala narrated Aisha's journey of seeking knowledge and her firm commitment to Islam, Reeda found herself mesmerised and influenced by the outstanding figure.

One day, something changed for Reeda. At first, she wasn't so keen on learning about deen, but then, she got genuinely interested. She began asking lots of questions about Islamic teachings and started to understand them better. The tough exterior she had was slowly going away.

Romana Khala, with her calm guidance and wise words during the classes, really helped Reeda. It wasn't just about the lessons; it was like a lightbulb moment for her. This change didn't just stay in the classes; it came home. Our place became more open to talking about Islam.

In one of their talks, I overheard Romana Khala saying, "Reeda, Islam is like a garden. Each lesson is like a flower. The more you understand, the more beautiful your garden becomes."

Reeda replied, "But sometimes it feels hard to understand everything." Romana Khala smiled and said, "That's okay. Learning is like taking small steps. Each step brings you closer to the beauty of the garden."

These talks weren't just about rules; they were like stories. Romana Khala shared stories about Prophet Muhammad (PBUH) and his companions. Reeda would ask, "Did the Prophet face tough times too?" Romana Khala nodded and said, "Yes, but his strong faith guided him through. Just like your faith can guide you."

Slowly, Reeda's curiosity turned into a love for learning about Islam. It wasn't just in our home; it spread like a good vibe around our neighbourhood. Romana Khala's way of teaching wasn't just about facts; it was about making Islam a part of our lives, like a friend you can always turn to.

These simple talks, the stories, and the lessons made our home a place where we could freely talk about Islam. It wasn't a serious thing; it was more like having a chat with a friend. And in those chats, Reeda found something beautiful – a connection with her faith that was genuine and growing, like a little seed turning into a strong tree.

This was the beginning of her being intensely devoted to Islam and practice 'Sunnah' and teaching us to do the same was an achievement for the elders in our family.

My sister was a highly motivated person, fearing Allah, and always had the confidence to handle difficult situations with courage. Her practice included saying 'Bismillah' before initiating every situation, whether it was holding a pen or opening a suitcase. I always heard her whispering 'Astagfirullah' every time she was free from any talks or work at home or outside. These made me feel proud of her every time I encountered her.

# THIS SIDE, ABRAR!

# 4

Hey, I'm Abrar, the guy who always had a joke up his sleeve, especially when it came to dealing with my little sister, Reeda. Our house was always filled with laughter, and I took it upon myself to be the official joke cracker.

Now, let me take you back to those days when fights between Reeda and me were as common as the sunrise. One time, we argued about who gets the TV remote. She said, "I was watching something!" I replied, "Well, I'm watching something now!" The debate continued until 'Amma' intervened with her classic line, "Share or no TV for both of you!"

The other day, feeling like a culinary genius, I decided to organize a 'Super Chef' pizza night. The plan was simple – everyone creates their own pizza masterpiece. Reeda, eying the array of toppings, asked skeptically, "Are you sure this won't turn into a disaster, Chef Abrar?"

Brushing off her concerns with a flourish, I replied, "Disaster? No way! Get ready for a pizza party of epic proportions!"

As we started, things got crazy. Tomato sauce splattered, cheese flew in unexpected directions, and toppings ended up in a colorful mishmash. Reeda, holding a rather unique pizza creation, couldn't help but laugh. "Chef, I think we've invented a new cuisine!"

Still proud of my 'Super Chef' vision, I declared, "It's not a disaster; it's fancy pizza art!"

Few days passed but in a burst of scientific curiosity, I decided to conduct a home science experiment involving baking soda and vinegar volcanoes. Reeda, witnessing my setup, raised an eyebrow and asked, "Are you sure this won't end with an explosion, Professor Abrar?"

With the confidence of an insane scientist, I retorted, "Explosion? Nonsense! This is groundbreaking science!"

As the vinegar met the baking soda, the 'volcano' erupted, but not in the controlled manner I had envisioned. Foam cascaded over the table, and Reeda, shielding herself, teased, "Professor Abrar, your volcano needs a safety warning!"

Ignoring the mess, I proudly stated, "It's not an explosion; it's an educational eruption!"

All these funny adventures made our home a place full of laughter and experiments. Even though things got messy, our strong bond kept growing. Each mess became a story, a memory in our crazy family life.

However, everything changed after she started learning about Islam. From a notorious kid, always ready for a quick argument or mischief, she transformed into a calm, patient person taking Islam seriously. It wasn't just about fights or petty arguments anymore; it was about understanding, patience, and a journey of growth. We all grew up, not just in age but in the way we approached life, thanks to the positive changes Reeda brought into our home through her newfound understanding of Islam.

# ABRAR'S BONDING WITH REEDA:

# 5

## A PROTECTIVE BROTHER'S TALE.

I always felt a strong sense of responsibility for Reeda, my younger sister. We shared a bond that went beyond just being siblings; it was a connection of trust and protection.

One day in the lively streets of Kashmir, where marketplaces hummed with the vibrancy of culture, Reeda and I set out for a routine shopping escapade. The air was filled with the aromatic blend of spices, and the narrow lanes were adorned with beautiful handicrafts that showcased the essence of Kashmiri life. Reeda and I went shopping for some essentials.

As we strolled through the crowded market, I couldn't help but notice the glances some men were giving her. It bothered me, not just because she was my sister, but because she was trying her best to observe the hijab, even if her face wasn't fully covered.

Feeling the need to shield her from unwanted attention, I approached Reeda and said, "Let's stick together, alright? It's crowded, and I want to make sure you're comfortable."

Reeda, sensing my protective stance, smiled and replied, "Thanks, Abrar. I appreciate it."

As we continued our shopping, the glances from some men persisted. Unable to hold back, one of them approached us and remarked, "Your sister is quite beautiful, my friend."

Reeda, sensing my concern, replied, "I'm fine, Abrar. Let's just get what we need."

Feeling my protective instincts kick in, I retorted, "She's off-limits. Move along."

He smirked, "Just appreciating beauty, man."

Reeda, noticing my tension, tugged at my sleeve, "Abrar, let it go. Not worth it."

But another guy chimed in, "You're lucky, having a sister like that."

I gritted my teeth, "Watch your words, or there'll be trouble."

Reeda, sensing a brewing storm, pleaded, "Abrar, please. Let's just finish shopping."

One guy, seemingly looking for a fight, shoved me. That was it. I stepped forward, ready to throw a punch, but Reeda grabbed my arm, "Abrar, no! It's not worth it."

I hesitated, caught between protecting my sister and causing a scene. Reeda's eyes pleaded with me to walk away. "Let's go, Abrar. Don't let them ruin our day."

Reluctantly, I turned away, anger boiling inside. As we left the market, Reeda whispered, "Thanks for not making it worse, Abrar."

I sighed, "They're not worth it, Reeda. But no one messes with you while I'm around."

It ended with a mix of frustration and relief. The incident highlighted the challenge of balancing protection and avoiding unnecessary trouble. But in the end, Reeda's words echoed in my mind – family came first, even when faced with unwarranted attention.

That incident reinforced the importance of our bond. In the face of adversity, my role as a protective brother became clear, and our mutual understanding deepened. Our journey continued, marked by these moments that strengthened the unspoken connection between us.

That day hit me hard when I realised the fact that time keeps moving, and I'll soon have to say bye to my sister as she will get married soon. It's like feeling happy for her next step but sad for the parting.

# THE INTERVIEW

# 6

The air in Kashmir was biting, each breath turning into a visible puff of mist as I passed through the snow-laden streets on my way to the interview.

The snow fell gently, making everything look beautiful and white. But despite the scenic surroundings, I felt super nervous. My eyes quickly looked at the huge snow-covered mountains around. I couldn't help biting my lower lip, a sign of my nervousness. The soft bites on my lower lip betrayed my anxiety.

Entering the building, the warmth was a stark contrast to the cold outside. I took a deep breath, gathering my composure before stepping into the interview room. The panel of interviewers sat across the table, their expressions scrutinising. Among them was Rayan, a face from my past, now a figure of authority. I hadn't anticipated this twist.

As I began to showcase my portfolio, the room echoed with the tapping of Rayan's pen against the table. "Tell us about your experience with content creation," he said, his eyes focused but betraying a hint of recognition.

I hunted deep into my journey, recounting the first project that set the course for my career. It was a freezing winter much like today, I began, stealing a glance at the snowy scene outside the window. My first day at a new office, I was eager but nervous. The receptionist handed me a project brief, and I dove right in.

As I told the story, I could see the memories clearly in my mind. The job was tough, but I was determined. "I worked all day, creating content, hoping it would be good. I didn't realise then how much it would matter."

Rayan stopped writing and leaned in, saying, "Keep going, tell me more."

"On that very day, I submitted my work, not expecting much. To my surprise, the head of the department was impressed and I got to work with them as a freelancer.", I replied.

There was a quiet moment in the room as I shared the surprising news. Rayan's eyes got big, and he smiled, saying, "Reeda?" like he couldn't believe it.

"Yeah, it's me," I said, feeling a mix of emotions.

He chuckled, a nostalgic glint in his eyes. "I can't believe it. We used to dream big about our futures, and here you are, walking into my office."

The tension in the room melted away, replaced by a shared history that bridged the years. "I had no idea you were behind all this," I admitted.

"Life takes unexpected turns," Rayan said, his gaze thoughtful. "But it looks like fate brought you here today."

The interview turned into a chat where we remembered the times when we were just kids dreaming big. Rayan told me how he started the company, and I was amazed at the journey that led us to this point.

"So, Reeda," Rayan said with a smile, "how about working with me as a part of this team?"

The offer hung in the air, and I couldn't help but grin. "I'd be honoured," I replied, feeling a surge of gratitude and excitement.

As we sealed the deal with a handshake, the snow outside continued its gentle descent, framing the scene with a touch of magic. The winter chill that had gripped me earlier transformed into a warmth that radiated from the realisation that sometimes, life comes full circle, reconnecting us with our past in unexpected ways.

And so, in the heart of Kashmir's winter, amidst the snowflakes and memories, a new chapter unfolded – a reunion of childhood friends turned colleagues, bound by a shared passion for storytelling and a future waiting to be written.

Few weeks later…

As we continued with our daily meetings in the office, Rayan and I found ourselves sharing more than just work updates. Our friendship deepened, and subtle glances turned into exchanged smiles. It was in those moments that something more than friendship began to blossom between us.

One day, after a particularly successful project, Rayan suggested we celebrate at a cozy restaurant by the serene Dal Lake. The atmosphere was perfect, with the shimmering water reflecting the warm glow of the city lights. As we sat there, discussing everything from dreams to childhood memories, an unspoken understanding remained in the air.

Amidst the soft sounds of the lake and the gentle breeze, Rayan looked at me with a warmth that went beyond friendship. "Reeda," he said, his voice filled with sincerity, "what if our dreams intertwine not just in work but in life too?"

I could feel my heart racing, understanding the feelings we had been avoiding. With a smile, I said,

"Why not? Let's make our dreams even more special together."

By the Dal Lake, under the stars, we decided to step into a new chapter. Our friendship had turned into something more, and we chose to face the future together. The restaurant by the lake became a special place, marking the start of a shared journey.

In the simple joy of sharing dreams and the decision made by the lake, our love story began, and our conversations turned into promises for a life together.

# THE HOSPITAL CORRIDOR

# 7

Rayan and I were knee-deep in planning our wedding, our minds often drifting away from the usual office tasks. We were on the verge of sharing our joy with our families when an unexpected disaster disrupted our lives. My brother, Umer, had met with a tragic accident while shooting videos for his budding vlogging channel in the landscapes of Pahalgam.

In the midst of our own plans, life threw us a curveball, reminding us of the saying, "Man plans, and God laughs." The accident added a layer of urgency and worry to our lives. Umer, who had always been passionate about computers, now harbored dreams of becoming a rider vlogger, aiming to carve a niche in the vast world of YouTube and earn a living through his newfound passion. It was a surprising turn of events, proving the quote that "men mature at the age of 42 unlike women."

On that chilly winter day, Umer, fueled by his new vlogging passion, set off for Pahalgam in Kashmir to capture the breathtaking landscapes for his YouTube channel. As he made through the winding roads, the excitement of the scenery was abruptly shattered. His motorcycle skidded on a patch of black ice, sending him crashing to the ground in the midst of snow-covered peaks and pine trees.

As Umer's motorcycle skidded on the treacherous mountain road, the sudden accident attracted the attention of passersby who swiftly dialed for assistance. In the hushed backdrop of snow-laden trees and the crisp winter air, the urgency to summon help created a sense of mystery and suspense.

An ambulance promptly arrived, its siren blending with the wintry wind as Umer was carefully loaded into it. The journey to Shifa Hospital in Srinagar began, through the narrow roads of Pahalgam and later into the bustling city. The once serene landscapes of Pahalgam transformed into a distant memory as the vehicle entered the busy streets.

Shifa Hospital, known for its medical expertise, rose against the cityscape, its entrance bustling with activity. The hospital, situated in Srinagar, a city celebrated for its vibrant markets and iconic houseboats floating on Dal Lake, now became an unexpected stage for a dramatic turn of events. The contrast between the hospital's sterile halls and the vivid life of Srinagar heightened the sense of drama. Inside the hospital, the medical team worked diligently to assess and address Umer's injuries. The hospital's corridors, typically filled with routine medical efforts, now housed a mysterious chapter in the daily rhythm of healing.

As Umer grappled with his recovery, the incident remained a poignant episode in the hospital's narrative. The resilience of Srinagar and its people, interwoven with the drama of Umer's accident, created a backdrop that echoed the unpredictable nature of life against the historical canvas of the city.

In the silent corridors of the hospital, amidst the hushed tones of medical staff and the distant hum of machinery, I stumbled upon a turning point that would shatter the tranquility I had desperately sought. Rayan, ostensibly there to support me during Umer's recovery, was engrossed in a phone conversation that would reveal a painful truth.

As I walked along the sterile hallway, the muffled conversation echoed through the quiet night. The lack of people around accentuated every word that reached my ears. Rayan's voice, usually warm and reassuring, now held a strained undertone. I overheard snippets of a woman's voice on the other end, sharp and accusatory.

In the one-sided conversation, Rayan attempted to calm the escalating tension. "I told you, I can't make it tonight," he pleaded, his words bouncing off the sterile walls. The woman's frustration, however, persisted, each word slicing through the air. "It's a big day for me,

Rayan! Why can't you understand?" she exclaimed, desperation evident in her tone.

As I continued down the corridor, the intensity of the conversation escalated. Rayan's attempts at explanation seemed feeble, and the woman's grievances grew louder. It was a surreal moment, the stark contrast between the life-saving efforts inside the hospital rooms and the emotional turmoil playing out through the unseen dialogue. In the midst of the escalating tension, there was a sudden shift. Rayan's voice, now softer, uttered words that sent a chill down my spine. "I love you," he confessed, the declaration hanging in the air, a painful revelation that reverberated through the quiet hospital night.

The impact of those three words remained as I grappled with the realisation that the person I trusted, who stood beside me during a family crisis, had a hidden chapter. The hospital's sterile walls seemed to close in, echoing not just the beeping of machines but the echoes of a shattered trust. The night, once filled with the promise of recovery and hope, now bore witness to a different kind of healing—one that involved mending a heart that had unexpectedly cracked in the silent corridors of the hospital.

In the long corridor of the hospital, the weight of what I had overheard pressed down on me as I approached Rayan. His face, previously a source of comfort, now held a subtle tension. The air was thick with unspoken words as I mustered the courage to confront him about the shocking phone call.

"Rayan," I said, my voice steady but laced with the tremors of disbelief, "who was that on the phone? What's going on?"

He looked at me, his eyes momentarily avoiding mine before meeting them with a forced calm. "It's just a misunderstanding, Reeda. Nothing to worry about."

His attempt to dismiss the conversation only fueled my concern. "A misunderstanding?" I retorted, unable to contain the frustration building within me. "I heard it all, Rayan. Don't insult my intelligence."

The hospital's sterile surroundings amplified the tension as I pressed for an explanation. "Who was she? What was that argument about?"

Rayan's expression shifted, a mix of guilt and evasion. "It's complicated, Reeda. She's someone from the past, but it doesn't change what we have."

The words hung in the air, heavy with uncertainty. "Complicated?" I repeated, my disbelief turning into a painful reality. "You said 'I love you' to her, Rayan. How is that just complicated?"

His eyes, avoiding mine, finally met my gaze. The silence between us was deafening, the emotional turbulence in that sterile corridor mirroring the chaos within me. I needed answers, clarity, but what I received was a silence that spoke volumes.

Finally, with a heavy sigh, Rayan admitted, "Reeda, I messed up. I should have been honest with you from the start. It's someone I cared about before, but it's over now. I love you."

The confession, couldn't erase the pain.

In the quiet hospital hallway, everything felt different after I confronted Rayan about the phone call. The air felt heavy with the truth that he'd confessed. I was trying to understand what had happened, but it felt like a lot to carry. The future between us looked unclear, and finding a way to move forward seemed tough because of the hurtful betrayal I had just learned about.

# REEDA'S JOURNAL

# 8

## ***D*ear Diary,**

*The crisp pages bear witness to a night of revelations that has left my heart heavy. In the quiet aftermath of the hospital corridors, I am pouring my emotions onto these blank spaces.*

*The ink on the paper mirrors the uncertainty that now lingers in my life. Rayan's confession echoes in my mind, each word etching itself onto my heart. The trust we shared has been replaced by the shadows of betrayal, and I struggle to make sense of the path that lies ahead.*

*Every stroke of the pen is like a cry from my soul, trying to make sense of the hurt I'm feeling.*

*The pages, once blank and full of dreams, now show the scars of a love that's broken. My words on this paper are a river of tears, tracing the pain in my heart.*

*I'm struggling to understand a reality that doesn't match the dreams I had. This diary, my secret keeper, is where I pour out the trauma, the pain that feels like a storm inside me.*

*As I write, I face the shadows of a love that promised warmth but gave me a cold betrayal.*

*With every word, I untangle the mess of emotions, allowing myself to bleed onto the paper. The pen is like a lifeline, helping me hold myself together in the face of wounds that threaten to break me.*

*In this dance of ink and feelings, I'm confronting the deep hurt, one step at a time. The diary becomes a place for my tears, witnessing the pain of a heart that once knew only love. In these pages, I share my struggles and try to make sense of a reality that feels like a harsh illusion.*

*The ink bears the scars of my pain, and with each word, my emotions threatens to consume me whole.*

*– Reeda Reshi*

# UNDER THE ROOF OF THE RESHI FAMILY

# 9

Mrs. Reshi: You know, Reeda is at that age where we should start thinking about her marriage.

Mr. Reshi: Yes, it has crossed my mind. She's grown into a wonderful woman.

Mrs. Reshi: I've noticed her growing distant lately. Maybe finding a life partner could bring her joy.

Mr. Reshi: True. We want what's best for her. Have you thought about anyone in particular?

Mrs. Reshi: Well, Bilal has been a close friend for a long time. He's been there for Reeda in many ways.

Mr. Reshi: Ahem! Yeah, Bilal is a good person, and he knows our family well. But, do you think Reeda sees him in that way?

Mrs. Reshi: It's hard to say. I sense a connection between them, but we can't push her into anything.

Mrs. Reshi: Yes, let's be open with her. Marriage is a significant decision, and she deserves to have a say in it.

Mr. Reshi: Insha'Allah, we'll guide her through this with love and understanding.

Mrs. Reshi: May Allah bless her with a partner who brings joy to her life.

Mr. Reshi: Ameen. And may this be a new chapter filled with happiness for our Reeda.

Mrs. Reshi: Summa Ameen but Reeda seems very low nowadays.

Mr. Reshi: Yes, I've seen it too. Before we talk about marriage, we need to understand what's bothering her.

Mrs. Reshi: Perhaps there's something on her mind that she's not sharing. You've noticed it too, haven't you? Reeda has been so quiet lately. It's unsettling.

Mr. Reshi: Yes, it's been on my mind. I can't shake the feeling that something is troubling her.

Mrs. Reshi: She left her job, just like that, without any notice. Her passion for it seemed unbreakable.

Mr. Reshi: I remember how she used to light up when she talked about her work. It's like that spark has dimmed.

Mrs. Reshi: And she was so good at it! But now, it's like she's lost interest. I can't help but worry about what's going on inside her heart.

Mr. Reshi: Our Reeda has always been strong, though. Remember when she found that injured bird in the backyard as a child?

Mrs. Reshi: Oh, yes! She was so determined to nurse it back to health. Those were simpler times.

Mr. Reshi: And her storytelling! Those evenings filled with laughter and imagination. Haha!

Mrs. Reshi: Remember the incident when Reeda was about ten? It left her so disturbed.

Mr. Reshi: Ah, yes. It was that incident at school, wasn't it?

Mrs. Reshi: She came home in tears, barely able to speak. When she finally did, it was about an incident with some classmates, something that had hurt her deeply.

Mr. Reshi: I remember the pain in her eyes. She was bullied, and it shook her to the core.

Mrs. Reshi: We tried to console her, but it was affecting her so much. That's when we decided to take her to a psychologist.

Mr. Reshi: Dr. Khan. He was really good with her. Helped her process the pain and taught her how to cope.

Mrs. Reshi: It took time, but Reeda became stronger through those sessions. I just hope this recent silence doesn't mean she's facing something similar now.

Mr. Reshi: If she is, we need to be there for her, just like we were back then.

Mrs. Reshi: Indeed. We can't let her face it alone. Allah knows what she's going through. May He guide her.

Mr. Reshi: Ameen. Let's hope we can help her find the strength to overcome whatever it is. Our Reeda deserves all the happiness in the world.

Reeda: (overhearing the conversation) Mom, Dad, may I join you?

Mrs. Reshi: Of course, 'meri jaan'. We were just talking about you.

Reeda: I heard you mentioning marriage, and I want you to know that I've been thinking about it too.

Mr. Reshi: Reeda, sweetheart, we want what's best for you. Is there someone you have in mind?

Reeda: (hesitates) Actually, no but Bilal and I have been known to each other since so many years and

Romana khala is a very humble person, so I am sure Bilal is the reflection of his mother and I don't mind rejecting him if he shows up with a marriage proposal.

Mrs. Reshi: (smiles) Bilal is a good young man and I knew my daughter's choice won't disappoint us. 'Subhan'Allah'.

Reeda: (not willingly) I feel... I feel good about it. He understands me, and I believe we can build a life together.

Mr. Reshi: That's important, Reeda. We want your happiness above all. If Bilal makes you happy, then we support your decision.

Mrs. Reshi: We just want you to be open with us and communicate. Marriage is a significant step, and your well-being matters the most.

Reeda: Thank you, Mom, Dad. I appreciate your understanding. I would like to move forward, In Sha Allah.

Mr. Reshi: May Allah bless this new journey for you both. We're here for you every step of the way.

Mrs. Reshi: Ameen. Let this chapter bring joy and fulfillment to both of you. Ameen.

The Reshi family embraces an open and understanding conversation about Reeda's decision to marry Bilal. Their support for her happiness shines through as they express their blessings and commitment to being there for Reeda and Bilal as they enter this new chapter in their lives.

# THE DAY BILAL ARRIVED

# 10

The Reshi household is filled with a warm ambiance as Reeda's family eagerly awaits the arrival of Bilal and his mother, Romana. The fragrance of freshly cooked food wafts through the air, and the living room is adorned with soft lighting and comfortable seating. The living room is beautifully decorated with soft, warm lighting and plush seating, creating a welcoming ambiance. Reeda, dressed in an elegant outfit, nervously glances at the clock, while her parents, Mr. and Mrs. Reshi, exchange smiles, waiting for their guests.

Bilal arrives with his mother, Romana, who is not only Bilal's mother but also a respected Alimah who once taught Reeda Quran and Islamic teachings. The atmosphere is a blend of excitement and a touch of nervous anticipation as the two families gather for this significant moment.

The doorbell rings, and the Reshi family welcomes Bilal and Romana into their home. They step in, carrying a basket of meticulously arranged flowers and traditional Kashmiri sweets. The fragrance of the blooms mingles with the delicious scents from the kitchen, adding to the festive atmosphere.

Greetings and smiles are exchanged as they all gather in the living room.

Reeda, dressed in the traditional Kashmiri pheran, greets Bilal and Romana with a warm smile. The room gets filled with the rich colors and patterns of Kashmiri decor.

Reeda: (offering kahwa) Assalamualaikum, Please, have a seat!

Bilal: Walaikum aslam, Shukriya, Reeda. (takes a sip) Delicious!

The room is filled with a mix of laughter and conversation as they all take their seats. Mr. and Mrs. Reshi, Bilal, and Romana engage in pleasant conversation.

As they settle, Romana gracefully steers the conversation towards common memories, reflecting on the time she spent teaching Reeda Quran and Islamic teachings. This initiates a conversation that not only focuses on the past but also sets the stage for discussions about the future.

Romana: (addressing Reeda) It warms my heart to see the fine young woman you've become. I remember our Quran lessons with fondness.

Reeda: (grateful) Your teachings have been a guiding light, Romana.

The conversation naturally transitions into discussions about values, traditions, and the shared Islamic foundation that bonds the two families. Bilal expresses his admiration for Reeda's commitment to her faith, and the families find common ground in their shared values.

Bilal: (looking at Reeda) Your dedication to your faith has always been inspiring.

Reeda: (blushing) It's something I hold dear to my heart.

The atmosphere is marked by a genuine exchange of thoughts and aspirations.

On the other hand…

Rahi: (smirking) So, Bilal, we've heard a lot about you.

Bilal: (smiling) I hope it's all good things.

Abrar: We'll find out. (grinning) Rahi, why don't you start?

Rahi: Bilal, if you were a famous Kashmiri dish, which one would you be and why?

Bilal: (chuckles) Well, I'd say Yakhni. It's a blend of various flavors, just like life, and it brings warmth to those who savor it.

Razaq: (nodding) Not bad. Now, let's see how you handle this one. If you were caught in a traditional Kashmiri tug of war between winter and spring, which side would you choose?

Bilal: (thinking) I'd choose the transition, the moment when winter reluctantly gives way to the blossoming spring, a symbol of hope and new beginnings.

Umer: (smirking) Impressive. Now, for the tricky one. How would you describe your love for Reeda in the poetic style of Kashmiri folk songs?

Bilal: (smiling) Ah, that's a challenge. But I'd say, "Che yemberzal wuchhun, dilbar mye wuchhun," (Like the snow melting, my heart melts for you.)

The brothers exchange glances, nodding in approval.

Mrs. Reshi: (with a smile) Alhamdulillah.

Mr. Reshi: (raising an eyebrow) Well, you've passed the quiz, Bilal.

Bilal: (grinning) I'm honored.

Romana: (joining in) We're grateful for this warm welcome. Jazak Allah bhaijan.

As the evening progresses, the families continue to bond, and the atmosphere is filled with the joyous sounds of laughter and music. The brothers collectively say "Alhamdulillah," expressing their contentment and gratitude, signaling the approval of Bilal for Reeda.

Mr. Reshi: (shaking hands with bilal) Alhamdulillah, for this union and the joy it brings. Let us fix the date for this 'alishaan' celebration!

The scene concludes with the families joyously planning and fixing the date for the marriage in the authentic way of a Kashmiri wedding.

# THE NIKAAH

# 11

In the days leading up to the wedding, the Reshi household is alive with excitement. Reeda, joined by her mother and friends, goes shopping in the lively Kashmir markets. They select beautiful fabrics, intricate jewellery, and delicate accessories, for Reeda's special day.

Mrs. Reshi: (smiling) Reeda, you look so lovely in this Kashmiri outfit. It's just perfect for the Mehndi ceremony.

Reeda: (blushing) Thanks, Mom. I really want everything to be nice.

Back at home, Mr. Reshi and his sons are busy turning the house into a festive space. They hang colorful lights, put up decorations, and fill the air with the delicious aroma of Kashmiri dishes.

Mr. Reshi: (checking the decorations) Great job, everyone. The house is going to be full of joy.

However, a small disagreement arises between the brothers, Abrar and Umer, as they work on the final touches.

Abrar: (holding decorations) Umer, I think these bright colors will make the whole place come alive.

Umer: (disagreeing) No, Abrar. I think a simpler color scheme would be more elegant.

Abrar: (firmly) Elegant is good, but we need some excitement. It's a celebration, after all.

Umer: (firmly) I don't want it to be too much. Let's keep it simple and nice.

The disagreement gets a bit tense, but their father steps in to find a compromise.

Mr. Reshi: Abrar, Umer, let's find a middle ground. We want a celebration that's both classy and lively.

The brothers, understanding the need for agreement, work together to blend their ideas. The house transforms into a joyful space, reflecting the happiness of the upcoming wedding.

As the final touches are put in place, the Reshi household stands as a symbol of togetherness, showcasing a mix of styles and ideas—a perfect setting for the beautiful union on the horizon.

On the night before Reeda's Kashmiri wedding, her house is filled with activity, with everyone preparing for the big day. The air is filled with the delicious smell of traditional Kashmiri food, and the decorations make the house look festive. Despite the joy around her, Reeda takes a quiet moment alone.

Sitting with her beautiful wedding outfit, memories from the past flood Reeda's mind. The room, lit by soft candlelight, brings back moments of laughter with her brothers, talks with friends, and the warmth of family gatherings. She realises that life is about to change, and tears well up in her eyes.

Reeda moves to a quiet corner, hiding her emotions behind the folds of her colourful dress. Silent tears roll down her cheeks as she recalls cherished moments.

In this emotional moment, Reeda's mom enters the room, sensing her daughter's struggle. Worried, she gently asks what's on Reeda's mind.

Mrs. Reshi: (softly) Reeda, my love, what's bothering you?

Surprised, Reeda quickly wipes her tears, putting on a fragile smile.

Reeda: (trying to sound okay) Oh, Mom, I was just thinking about the 'Ruksati' tomorrow, leaving the home I've known.

Mrs. Reshi: (comforting her) It's okay, dear. 'Ruksati' is a mix of happiness and sadness. We're gaining a son, but you'll always be our precious daughter.

Reeda feels better after talking with her mom and getting a hug. The room, which felt full of memories without words, now feels different. Reeda and her mom understand each other as they get ready for the wedding. The night before the wedding is not just a time to think but also a time to feel the strong connection between Reeda and her mom, showing how family ties continue through the years.

On the morning of Reeda's wedding, everyone was getting ready for the big day. Suddenly, a message popped up on their phones. It said, "Bilal Ahmed, a local from Kashmir, found hung on a tree in Baramullah."

Shock and disbelief rippled through the room. Reeda, still in her bridal attire, stared at the screen, her joyous anticipation replaced by a sudden, chilling reality. The room, which moments ago was alive with celebration, became silent as the weight of the news sank in. Reeda, still in her wedding clothes, stared at the news.

Mrs. Reshi: (gasping) 'Ya Rabb' No! this can't be true.

Abrar, looking shocked, tried to comfort his mom.

Abrar: Bilal was just with us yesterday. How did this happen?

Reeda, in her bridal dress, couldn't hold back tears.

Reeda: (softly) Bilal... no.

Mr. Reshi, hearing the news, entered the room, and his face turned grave.

Mr. Reshi: What's going on? Why is everyone so quiet?

Mohsin Chacha, Reeda's paternal uncle, broke the news.

Mohsin Chacha: Bilal, the young man who was like family, is no more.

Mr. Reshi's face registered shock and grief.

Mr. Reshi: (voice trembling) No, this can't be happening.

Rahi, Reeda's brother, struggled to process the news.

Rahi: 'Ya Allah rehem!'

The room, once filled with celebration, transformed into a space heavy with sorrow. The Reshi family, usually so joyous, now faced the painful reality of Bilal's sudden departure, leaving them in a sombre and emotional state.

As they tried to understand, it came out that Bilal had a secret mission. Despite being born and raised in Kashmir, Bilal had been secretly involved in a mission with Pakistan. His double life, known to very few, became a revelation in the wake of his tragic end.

Authorities uncovered that Bilal had been working as an undercover operative, feeding information from within the local community to an external force. The complexity of his life, the intricate web of secrets, and the reasons behind his involvement left everyone grappling with a profound sense of betrayal and confusion.

In the silent valleys of Kashmir, Bilal Ahmed's life took an unexpected turn. Born and raised in the heart of the conflict, Bilal grew up witnessing the struggles and complexities that defined the region. Without anyone realising, Bilal got involved in a hidden mission.

Bilal's story starts in college when he met someone mysterious. This person promised Bilal a chance to make a difference in his hometown. Intrigued by this cause, Bilal joined a secret group working for what they believed was a greater good. His life became a juggling act between normal days and undercover nights. In the day, he was a friendly face, laughing with friends and being close to family. At night, he turned into a secret agent, dealing with a web of hidden information. In the middle of this secret life, Bilal fell in love with Reeda. Getting married made him want to escape from the hidden world he got trapped in. Struggling between loyalty and the wish for a normal life, Bilal made a risky plan to break free from his mysterious handlers. As his wedding day got closer, the group he wanted to leave found out about his plans. They thought his decision to get married was a betrayal that could ruin their secret work. In a scary twist, Bilal was caught, and those against him saw him as a problem to be dealt with.

Therefore, on the morning of the wedding, everyone heard the sad news that Bilal had died. He was discovered hanging from a tree in Baramulla. This was a harsh outcome because he tried to escape from the secret group. The love story that seemed full of hope got mixed up in a complicated mess of spying, betrayal, and the difficulties of living two lives at once.

Bilal's story is like a puzzle of love and hidden truths in the troubled region. It teaches a lesson about the unexpected problems that can arise when you live in the shadows. The valleys of Kashmir, carrying the stories of the past, hide the untold journey of a man who tried to fix things but got caught up in the complexities of a life where loyalty and deceit mix at the borderlands.

A journalist's tweet pops up on Abrar's phone which read:-

'Bilal's story teaches us that the choices we make, even if we think they're for a good reason, can have unexpected and serious results. His secret mission caused a lot of problems, showing how complicated life can get when we keep things hidden. The lesson is to think about the consequences of our decisions and to be open and honest in our relationships, avoiding secrets that might lead to sad outcomes. It's a reminder to be careful and considerate in the choices we make.'

Abrar, seeing the tears streaming down Reeda's face, rushed to her side. Without a word, he enveloped her in a tight hug, providing a comforting embrace as if to shield her from the weight of the heartbreaking news. The vibrant colours of Reeda's bridal attire seemed to blend with the subdued hues of their shared sorrow.

Abrar: (softly) We're here for you, Reeda. I can't imagine how you're feeling, but we'll get through this. Please stop crying.

Reeda: (crying) Abrar, I can't believe this is happening. Why is fate so cruel? Everything was supposed to be happy today.

Abrar: Sometimes life throws challenges our way, and we can't control everything. It's not your fault.

Reeda: (sighs) I feel like everything is falling apart. Why does it have to be like this?

Abrar: (hugging her tighter) I know it's tough, Reeda. But blaming yourself or fate won't change what happened. We have to support each other.

Reeda: (voice trembling) I can't stop thinking about death, Abrar. It's like everything is so dark.

Abrar: (softly) I understand it's hard. But we can find light together. Let's not focus on the darkness. We're a family, and we'll face whatever comes our way, okay?

Reeda: (crying out loud) I just wish Bilal was here. It's so unfair.

Abrar: Life can be unfair, but we'll remember him and find a way to keep going. You're not alone, Reeda.

Abrar spoke gently to Reeda, trying to comfort her. Their hug was like a safe place, a moment where their close bond helped them deal with the sadness. In that hug, Abrar wanted to show Reeda that they were strong together as a family, even when things were tough. It was a way of saying they would face problems side by side, no matter what happened.

# MASKED FACE

# 12

## Few months later...

Months had passed since Bilal's tragic end, and the Reshi family tried to go back to normal. The morning sun made the house look hopeful and warm.

The Reshi household, nestled in the heart of Kashmir, woke up to the soft melodies of chirping birds. Reeda, despite the passing months, still carried a silent burden that lingered in the corners of her smile.

In the morning, she moved through the routine with a smile that masked the disturbance within. Her parents, still grieving in their own ways, saw the outward cheerfulness and believed their daughter was coping well.

**Morning at the Reshi Home:**

Mr. Reshi: (cheerfully) Good morning, everyone! Reeda, come, have breakfast.

Reeda: (smiling) Morning, Baba. I'm coming.

Reeda joined the family at the breakfast table, her smile carefully crafted to reassure her parents.

Mrs. Reshi: (concerned) How did you sleep, beta?

Reeda: (brightly) Oh, just fine, Ammi. I had a good night.

Later in the day, the aroma of spices filled the atmosphere as Mrs. Reshi prepared Wazwan (a traditional Kashmiri meal).

Mrs. Reshi: (with a smile) Reeda, can you help me with the spices? You always have the magic touch.

Reeda: (grinning) Of course, Ammi. Anything for you.

Meanwhile, Reeda's father gets into the kitchen with apple cartons.

Mr. Reshi: How's work, beta?

Reeda: It's going well, Baba. I keep myself busy.

Mrs. Reshi: (noticing) Your smile seems different today. Are you okay?

Reeda: Just thinking about a blog, Ammi. Nothing to worry about.

Rahi: (teasing) Reeda, did you see the neighbour's cat again?

Reeda: (laughs) Yes, Rahi, it's become my morning companion.

Family: (together) Eid is approaching. We should plan something special.

Reeda: (unwillingly) Absolutely! We can invite Mohsin Chacha and his family. It's been a long time since we met them.

**The Family Over Dinner: -**

Mrs. Reshi: (smiling) Remember that time Rahi got stuck in the tree?

Rahi: (laughing) Oh, let's not bring that up again.

Reeda: (forcing a laugh) Yeah, that was hilarious.

Mr. Reshi: (grinning) And what about Reeda's adventurous hiking trip?

Reeda: (faking laughter) Ah, the less said about that, the better.

Rahi: (teasing) You were like a lost explorer!

Mrs. Reshi: (joining in) We laughed so much that day.

Rahi: (joking) Reeda, remember Abrar's attempt at cooking?

Reeda: (forcing a chuckle) Oh, yes. Quite the chef he thought he was.

As the family shared old stories, Reeda tried to join in their laughter, but inside, the pain stuck like a shadow. Her smile hid the discomfort she felt.

Reeda: (forcing a smile) It's nice to laugh with everyone.

Deep down, the memories brought both joy and a twinge of sadness for Reeda. She wanted to be part of the happiness but couldn't shake off the heaviness within. Her smile, though sincere, carried the weight of unspoken struggles.

After dinner, Reeda said she was tired and went to her room, closing the door. In the quiet darkness, she felt a different kind of pain, not physical but inside her heart.

In the quiet and dark room, she confronted the memories of what happened. Tears fell silently, marking her pillow as the heavy feelings of sorrow and hidden emotions become overwhelming. The burden became too hard for her to handle.

She couldn't bring herself to burden her family with her inner struggle, so she wore a mask of normalcy during the day. The night, however, became a battleground for her mental health. The pain, though invisible to others, was a silent scream echoing in the solitude of her room. Despite the facade of a smile during the day, Reeda's nights were a stark contrast, revealing the rawness of her struggle to come to terms with the tragedy that had reshaped her world. The journey to heal was far from over, and the shadows behind her smile spoke of battles fought in the silent depths of the night.

In the middle of the night, Reeda wakes up abruptly and hurriedly goes to her laptop. She logs into her website where she had posted a poem about Bilal the night before their wedding. The poem, titled "My Kashmiri Husband," expresses deep love and admiration for Bilal's character and charm.

She reads the poetry softly to herself which was:

**My Kashmiri Husband**

In Kashmir's chest, my heart does reside,
A handsome soul, with charm as his pride.
With genuine grace and warmth so rare,
He ignites my heart with a loving flare.

His laughter echoes in the mountain's air,
A sense of humour beyond compare.
Finance analyst by trade and by heart,
Yet an artist's vision, a work of art.
When trust faltered, his light shone through,
Guiding my heart, skies turned from grey to blue.
Charming and kind, his personality so true,
In his presence, old wounds bid adieu.

With every roast, a playful delight,
He warms my heart, every day and night.
In Kashmir's realm, where beauty blooms,
Stands my lover, a masterpiece in rooms.

Through trust's dark fog, he cast a light,
His charm is a source of survival in the night.
From doubt's abyss, he pulled me near,
His genuine soul, wiping every tear.

A beautiful soul, wise and keen,
Yet in his eyes, an artist's dream.
Kashmiri grace, a heart so true,
In his embrace, my love did brew.
With care, trust, and eyes of art,
He captured my precious heart.

To my Kashmiri love, a tale untold,
A genuine gem with a heart of gold.
With humour and trust, he's set me free,
A masterpiece of love, just he and me.

As she reads the verses, the contrasting feelings intensify. The poetry becomes a heart-rending reminder of love lost, and tears start to flow down Reeda's face. With a heavy heart, she moves the cursor to the right bottom of the screen, revealing three options. Clicking on them, she chooses the irreversible action – "Delete Permanently."

A confirmation message pops up, asking if she's sure about this choice. Hovering over the "OK" button, Reeda takes a moment, caught in the internal struggle reflected on the screen. After a deep breath, she decides to go ahead and clicks "OK." The poem, once a source of relief, disappears from the digital space, symbolizing a significant step in letting go of the past. The night continues, quieter now, as Reeda grapples with the profound act of moving forward on her healing journey.

# MISSION ALIGARH

# 13

The very next day, a jingling of keys announced Mohsin Chacha's arrival at Reeda's house.

He brought more than just casual conversation—he had a brochure in hand, hinting at a purposeful visit. As he entered, Reeda, tucked away in a quiet corner, looked up with a hint of curiosity.

Mohsin Chacha: (with a playful smile) "Assalamu Alaikum, Reeda! I've got news that might spice up your routine."

Reeda: (intrigued) "Wa Alaikum Assalam, Chacha.

Tui chiv thik? (How are you?) News? What's it about?"

With a touch of drama, Mohsin Chacha revealed the brochure, presenting it as though it held secrets unreleased.

Mohsin Chacha: "Aa Alhamdulillah (Yes I am good) Ever thought about trying out the charm of Aligarh? A new adventure, perhaps?"

Caught off guard by the unexpected twist, Reeda leaned in to inspect the brochure. The images of Aligarh's lively atmosphere and its prestigious university piqued her interest.

Reeda: "Aligarh? What's there for me?"

Mohsin Chacha: "How about pursuing B.Ed? A change of scenery might be just what you need. There's a good college in Aligarh. Who knows what opportunities it might open for you?"

Reeda's eyes lit up with a mix of surprise and interest. The idea of a fresh start, presented in this unique way, injected a newfound excitement into the conversation. Aligarh wasn't just a destination for studies; it became the canvas where Reeda could begin painting her journey of rediscovery.

The air carried the inviting scent of freshly brewed kehwa as Mr. and Mrs. Reshi stepped into the room, infusing it with a welcoming warmth. Umer, the spirited younger brother, joined in, bringing a lively energy that set the tone for an unexpected family gathering. The table, adorned with an assortment of dry fruits, hinted at an impromptu feast. Laughter and chatter filled the room as they settled in, creating a familiar ambiance of shared moments.

In the midst of this familial warmth, Mohsin Chacha, holding a mysterious brochure, playfully raised his cup of kehwa, sparking curiosity among the family members.

Mohsin Chacha: (raising his cup) "To new beginnings and endless possibilities in Aligarh!"

Mr. Reshi: "Aligarh? What's this all about, Mohsin?"

Mohsin Chacha: "Well, how about we let Reeda herself share the exciting news? It's something that might bring a positive change."

The room buzzed with anticipation as Mohsin Chacha's words hung in the air. Umer, always the provocateur, couldn't resist a playful jab at Reeda.

Umer: (teasingly) "Reeda, are you planning to conquer Aligarh with your charm now?"

Reeda: (blushing) "Oh please, Umer. It's not like that."

Amidst the banter, the aroma of kehwa blended with the rich flavor of dry fruits, creating an atmosphere of familial warmth. The Reshi household became the stage for a significant revelation.

As the conversation continued to flow, Abrar, the eldest brother, joined the gathering, his presence infusing a sense of stability and wisdom.

Abrar: "Salaam, everyone! What's the buzz about Aligarh?"

Mohsin Chacha: "Abrar, you're just in time. We're discussing the prospect of Reeda pursuing her B.Ed in Aligarh."

Abrar: "That's great news! Reeda, this could be a fresh start for you."

The lunch table, set the scene for a more serious turn in the conversation. Mohsin Chacha, with a certain gravitas, guided the discussion towards Reeda's mental well-being.

Mohsin Chacha: (earnestly) "I believe this change can be transformative for Reeda. It's not just about studies; it's a chance for her to heal, to put the past behind."

In the midst of this profound discussion, Mrs. Reshi expressed a motherly concern, her eyes reflecting both love and worry.

Mrs. Reshi: "But will she be okay alone there?"

Mohsin Chacha: "She won't be alone. She'll make friends, find support. Sometimes, a change of environment can be therapeutic for mental health."

The room momentarily hushed, absorbing the weight of Mrs. Reshi's concern. Mohsin Chacha, sensing the need for reassurance, continued with a gentle conviction.

Mohsin Chacha: "I understand your concerns, but staying here might also keep her tied to the memories. Aligarh could offer her a fresh perspective."

As the conversation ebbed and flowed, the lunch table transformed into a white sheet where the Reshi family brushed their hopes, fears, and dreams for Reeda's future. Mohsin Chacha's words became a source of optimism, igniting a flicker of hope for a brighter tomorrow.

Umer: (jovially) "Well, Reeda, it seems like Aligarh is calling your name. Are you ready for this adventure?"

Reeda: (smiling) "I think I am. It's time for a new chapter."

Abrar: "Change is inevitable, and sometimes, it's the catalyst for growth. Reeda, we're with you every step of the way."

Throughout the lunch, the room was filled with laughter, conversations and discussions of the Reshi family. This created a strong sense of familial bonds, representing hope, and unending support. The interactions among family members contributed to a connected and supportive atmosphere. The common experiences portrayed understanding and encouragement within the family.

After a week, the entire family buzzed with activity as everyone gathered to prepare Reeda's luggage for her journey to Aligarh. Mrs. Reshi meticulously folded clothes, Mr. Reshi searched for suitable travel essentials, and Umer enthusiastically grabbed a notepad to jot down safety precautions for hostel life.

Mr. Reshi: "Make sure you have warm clothes, beta. Aligarh can get chilly."

Mrs. Reshi: "And pack some of your favorite snacks. You know how the hostel food might be."

Umer: "Don't forget a small toolkit. You never know when you might need it."

As they discussed the practicalities, Abrar entered the room, bringing with him a calming presence.

Abrar: "Reeda, here's a list of emergency contacts. Keep it handy, okay?"

Reeda: "Thanks, Abrar. You're all making me feel so supported."

While the focus was on preparations, the underlying emotions were palpable. Mohsin Chacha, observing the scene, interjected with a piece of advice.

Mohsin Chacha: "Reeda, remember to explore and embrace the new opportunities. Aligarh is a different world, but you have our blessings."

Mrs. Reshi: "And call us every day. Don't forget to stay connected."

The room became a hub of emotions and practicalities, a blend of love and preparation for a new chapter in Reeda's life. The family, though engaged in the logistics, shared moments that etched a sense of support and care into the fabric of her journey ahead.

Meanwhile Rahi and Reeda's father entered the room with few necessities.

Rahi: "Reeda, sweetheart, don't forget to be aware of your surroundings. If anything feels off, trust your instincts."

Mr. Reshi: "And carry a whistle. It might sound old-fashioned, but it can be a quick way to draw attention if you ever feel unsafe."

Reeda: "I'll remember, Baba. Thanks for looking out for me."

As they discussed safety measures, Rahi, with a reassuring smile, joined in.

Rahi: "Reeda, let me share a beautiful Hadith that might resonate with you. It's about the importance of modesty."

Mr. Reshi: "Yes, it's a valuable lesson for all of us."

Rahi began recounting the Hadith: "Prophet Muhammad (peace be upon him) said, 'Every religion has a distinct characteristic, and the distinct characteristic of Islam is modesty.'"

Reeda: "What does that mean, Rahi?"

Rahi: "It means that maintaining your modesty is not just a cultural thing; it's deeply rooted in our faith. It's a quality that sets us apart. Your modesty is a shield, protecting you from harm and preserving your dignity."

Mr. Reshi: "And remember, Reeda, the Prophet also said, 'Modesty brings nothing but goodness.'"

Reeda: "I understand. I'll keep that in my heart, Rahi and Baba."

In that moment, the Hadith became a guiding light, emphasizing the significance of modesty in Islam and encouraging Reeda to carry this strength with her on her journey.

Departure Scene at the Airport:

The departure gate rushed with the hurried footsteps of travelers, announcements echoing through the bustling terminal. Reeda, surrounded by her family, clutched her boarding pass, her eyes reflecting a mix of excitement and the bittersweet realization of leaving home.

Mrs. Reshi: "Take care, beta. Call us as soon as you land."

Umer: "Don't forget to WhatsApp us your first glimpse of Aligarh."

Reeda: "I'll miss you all. Jazakallah for everything."

At the departure gate, her family surrounded her, sharing last-minute advice and affectionate hugs. Mrs. Reshi reminded her to stay safe, while Umer, the playful younger brother, teased her about documenting her Aligarh journey on WhatsApp.

**In-Flight Experience:**

Seated by the window, She exchanged smiles with fellow passengers, struck up conversations, and found comfort in the shared experience of getting in on new beginnings.

Lost in the moment, she was fully immersed when she heard the flight attendant making an announcement for the first time:

*'Ladies and gentlemen, good morning. Welcome to Indigo flight 6E-123 bound for Aligarh.*

*Before we take off, we'd like to acquaint you with some safety features of this aircraft. First and foremost, please make sure your seatbelt is securely fastened low and tight across your lap. Insert the metal fitting into the buckle, and pull the strap so it's snug. To release, lift the top of the buckle.*

*There are six emergency exits on this aircraft, two at the front, two over the wings, and two at the rear. Please take a moment to locate the nearest exit. Keep in mind that the closest exit may be behind you.*

*In the event of a loss of cabin pressure, oxygen masks will drop from the overhead compartments. To start the flow of oxygen, pull the mask towards you. Place it firmly over your nose and mouth, secure it with the elastic band, and breathe normally. Make sure to adjust your mask before assisting others.*

*Smoking is not permitted on this aircraft, including in the lavatories. Federal law prohibits tampering with, disabling, or destroying any smoke detector in an aircraft lavatory.*

*Please ensure that all electronic devices are turned off during takeoff and landing, and set to airplane mode during the flight. Larger electronic devices should be stowed for departure.*

*Thank you for your attention. Sit back, relax, and enjoy your flight with us. If you have any questions or need assistance, don't hesitate to ask one of our crew members. Thank you.'*

Reeda watched as the plane ascended into the skies, bidding farewell to the familiar landscapes of Kashmir. The in-flight announcements and the hum of the engines created a background instrumental for her introspective thoughts.

As the aircraft descended towards Aligarh, Reeda's excitement reached its zenith. The flight attendants, like choreographers orchestrating a grand finale, prepared the cabin for the imminent landing. Through the aircraft window, the cityscape of Aligarh unfolded gradually, a patchwork of stories waiting to be discovered. The landing itself was a dance of precision, the wheels meeting the runway with a grace that echoed the official commencement of Reeda's Aligarh exciting journey.

Stepping off the plane, Reeda was met by the caress of Aligarh's warm breeze, a greeting that whispered promises of new beginnings. The mission her family had orchestrated, aptly named "Mission Aligarh," had transformed from familial discussions to a tangible, unfolding reality. The surface beneath her feet marked not just the end of a journey but the inauguration of a chapter yet to be written. With each step, Reeda clasped the pulsating energy of Aligarh, ready to write her new journey.

# ROOM 203

# 14

As Reeda stepped into the hostel, the corridor looked like a long hallway of possibilities. She found her room, marked with a big 203. Next door, laughter spilled out as the door swung open, revealing Jaspreet, her new roommate. Jaspreet was a lively girl with a big smile, making Reeda feel comfortable right away.

"Hey there! You must be my new neighbor!" Jaspreet exclaimed, her enthusiasm contagious. They sat on their beds, getting to know each other.

"Alright, new buddy, let's talk rules!" Jaspreet said with a grin. She shared, "Gate timings are like Cinderella's curfew here. Weekdays it's 10 pm, weekends 11 pm. Miss the deadline, and no magic carriage to sneak in."

As they laughed over the mischievous comparison, Jaspreet continued, "Now, meals are an event. Breakfast is a sunrise affair – be there by 8 am sharp. Lunch is at 1 pm, and dinner, our grand finale, kicks off at 7 pm. Punctuality is the secret sauce here! "And yeah our beloved warden, Mrs. Gupta, is like the hostel's Dumbledore. Strict but secretly rooting for us. She's got a keen eye, so no mischief on her watch!"

Reeda found comfort in Jaspreet's friendly guidance, turning what could have been an intimidating introduction into a shared laughter-filled exploration of their new home.

Reeda: (unpacking her belongings) So, Jaspreet, have you ever been to Kashmir?

Jaspreet: Oh, Kashmir! No, never been, but I've heard it's breathtaking. The Dal Lake, snow-capped mountains – must be like living in a postcard!

Reeda: (smiling) It truly is. The beauty is surreal. The landscapes, the Chinars – everything has a magical touch.

Jaspreet: (curious) Must be tough leaving all that behind. Why Aligarh?

Reeda: Well, family thought a change of scenery might help me heal. Plus, this college is renowned for education.

Jaspreet: (nodding) Makes sense. Sometimes a new place brings a fresh perspective. You'll love it here – we're like a big, crazy family.

Reeda: That's reassuring. Do you miss your home?

Jaspreet: A bit, but life here is a rollercoaster, and I love the ride. Besides, we're going to create some amazing memories together!

Reeda: (curious) Jaspreet, where are you from?

Jaspreet: (smiling) Ah, I'm from Punjab, the land of bhangra and butter chicken. Haha!

Reeda: You're hillarious! Anyways let's hit the sack. I need to rush to college tomorrow, it's my first day.

Jaspreet: yeah sure, lock your room properly before sleeping. Sleep tight kashmiran!

Reeda: What? How do you know this?

Jaspreet: I am a great stalker, people pays me for stalking people through their social media or if required through web for celeb figures like you. Write an autobiography on me too, someday. I believe you'll get content beyond your expectations.

Reeda: Haha! Very funny, go sleep. We'll continue some other day. Allah hafiz. Oops sorry! Sorry! By mistake. Actually I have developed a habit you know. I am really sorry.

Jaspreet: Take light love! Allah hafiz! Shabba khair! Haha!

# TULIP

# 15

The next morning at college, Reeda walked through the busy hallways, feeling a bit overwhelmed by all the new faces and the lively atmosphere. Some students hurried to their classes, chatting and laughing, creating a vibrant scene.

Aryan: Hey, are you new here?

Reeda: Yeah, just started.

Sarah: Welcome to the chaos! I'm Sarah, and this is Aryan. Nice to meet you.

Reeda: Thanks! I'm Reeda.

As they walked together towards the lecture hall, Reeda couldn't help but feel a sense of friendship. The morning sun rays lit up the campus, marking the beginning of her academic journey in Aligarh. The day unboxed with introductions, classes, and the exploration of this new chapter in her life.

In the bustling college canteen, Jaspreet joined Aryan, Sarah, and Reeda at a table, adding her infectious energy to the lively atmosphere.

Jaspreet: Hey, everyone! Mind if I join?

Aryan: Not at all. This is Reeda; she's new here.

Jaspreet: Awesome! Welcome, Reeda. As if I didn't meet you earlier! Haha! You're in for a treat; this canteen has the best chai.

Reeda: Ahm actually she's my roommate and we had already met each other in the hostel.

Aryan: Oh great, you're in safe hands now Reeda.

Sarah: So, Reeda, what brings you to Aligarh?

Reeda: Just started my B.Ed. here.

Jaspreet: B.Ed., huh? We've got ourselves an aspiring teacher. Nice choice!

As they chatted over cups of chai and snacks, the fellowship grew stronger, making the canteen a place filled with laughter and shared stories.

**In the room: -**

In the cosy confines of her hostel room, Reeda settled with her laptop, exhaustion persisting from the day's activities. As she opened the video call app, the familiar faces of her family greeted her on the screen.

Reeda: (smiling) Assalamu-Alaikum everyone! How's everything back home?

Mrs. Reshi: (excited) Walaikum aslam Reeda, beta! Look how your father has tried to cook your favourite dish today.

Mr. Reshi: (grinning) Well, I attempted. Your mother had to save the day, though.

Umer: (waving) Hey, lil sister! How's Aligarh treating you?

Reeda: (grateful) It's different, but good. Classes are intense, and the campus is huge.

Rahi: (enthusiastic) Tell us more. We want to know every detail.

Mrs. Reshi: (smiling) Guys stop it, let me talk to my daughter. So betaa, did you find everything okay? I hope your room is comfortable.

Reeda: Yes, Ammi, the room is fine. Jaspreet, my roommate, is quite friendly.

Mr. Reshi: (teasing) Any interesting classmates?

Reeda: (blushing) Dad! It's just the first day.

Umer: (playful) Any cute guys in Aligarh?

Reeda: (laughing) Umer, focus on your studies!

Rahi: (curious) How's the weather there? Kashmir must be colder.

Reeda: It's different. The evenings are pleasant.

Mrs. Reshi: (concerned) Are you eating properly? Don't skip meals.

Reeda: (nodding) No, Ammi, the hostel food is decent. I'm taking care of myself.

Umer: (mischievous) Remember, if you ever need snacks, I can send them by courier.

Reeda: (smiling) Thanks, Umer, but I'll manage.

Rahi: (reflective) Do you miss the mountains?

Reeda: (softly) A bit. But Aligarh has its charm.

Mr. Reshi: (wise) Focus on your studies, beta. This is a new chapter for you.

Reeda: (grateful) I will, Abbu. I want to make you all proud.

Umer: (excited) Any interesting professors?

Reeda: (enthusiastic) Yes, my English professor is really inspiring.

Rahi: (supportive) Remember, we're just a call away. If you ever feel overwhelmed, talk to us.

Reeda: (appreciative) I know, Rahi bhai. It means a lot.

Mrs. Reshi: (sentimental) We miss you, Reeda. Take care of yourself.

Reeda: (emotionally) I miss you all too. Love you.

As the conversation continued, the Reshi family bridged the distance with laughter, concern, and shared love through the pixels of a video call.

9

As soon as Reeda drops the call, Jaspreet hops in:

Jaspreet: Wow, Reeda! Your family seems so warm and lively. Tell me more about them.

Reeda: (smiling) Yeah, they're the heartbeat of my life. My parents are the pillars, my brothers bring the chaos, and together, we make a perfect mess.

Jaspreet: (enthusiastically) And that beautiful place you call home – Kashmir! Your house is beautiful. I heard Kashmiris are known for their hospitality. Your family reflects that.

Reeda: (nodding) Hospitality is deeply ingrained in our culture. Guests are treated like royalty, and the warmth of a cup of kahwa can make anyone feel at home.

Jaspreet: (intrigued) Kehwa? That's the traditional Kashmiri tea, right?

Reeda: Exactly! It's a blend of green tea, cardamom, and almonds. You should taste it someday; it's like a hug in a cup.

Jaspreet: (smiling) I'd love that. Your family seems so close-knit. Do you miss them?

Reeda: Every day. But thanks to technology, we bridge the distance. Video calls make it feel like they're just a heartbeat away.

Jaspreet: Your family seems lively! Anyways your brother was really good. The one teasing you.

Reeda: Oh, Umer is a character. Always full of energy, cracking jokes. He's got this dream of being a famous vlogger.

Jaspreet: Vlogger? Interesting! What's he vlogging about?

Reeda: Everything and anything. From Kashmir's breathtaking landscapes to his latest experiments in the kitchen.

Jaspreet: (laughs) Sounds like a fun guy. Do you think he'd be interested in a non-Muslim girl?

Reeda: (teasingly) Well, you'll have to convert to Islam for that to happen. Umer is quite strict about that.

Jaspreet: (playfully) Seriously? Does he have a checklist for potential sisters-in-law?

Reeda: (smirking) Oh, absolutely! Must love biryani, know how to dance to Kashmiri tunes, and most importantly, convert to Islam.

Jaspreet: (laughs) Well, I might need to work on my biryani skills.

Reeda: (jokingly) And the conversion part?

Jaspreet: (grinning) Let's not rush things, Reeda. I'm just starting to get used to the kehwa here.

They both burst into laughter, bonding over cultural differences and the humour that bridged them together in their new journey.

9

**Abrar's new chapter:-**

As I toiled away on my blog, Abrar's face popped up on the screen through a video call. The enthusiasm in his voice was contagious as he began, "Reeda, you won't believe what happened!" Intrigued, I listened attentively.

Abrar's eyes sparkled with joy as he shared, "I found the girl of my dreams on Twitter. She's this incredible Bengali Muslim with a passion for writing like you. Reeda, her beauty isn't just in her appearance, but in the kindness that radiates from her soul. Her eyes hold a universe of stories, and when she smiles, it's like the world lights up."

As he continued, each word painted a portrait of her – a woman of substance, intelligence, and warmth. I couldn't help but smile at his animated description. "She's passionate about her values and beliefs, and our conversations go beyond the surface. It's like we've known each other for a lifetime, despite the miles that separate us," Abrar exclaimed, his excitement palpable.

In that moment, I witnessed my brother's heart blooming with affection for someone who seemed to bring out the best in him. The way he spoke of her was more than admiration; it was an acknowledgment of a connection that transcended screens and distances.

Abrar elaborated on the challenges and commitment of a long-distance connection. As he described her, I felt genuinely happy for him. Despite the distance, their bond seemed strong and that was the moment I realised the power of modern love, where relationships could thrive despite physical separation.

**From the journal of Reeda**

# MYSELF JASPREET!

# 16

Within the hallowed halls of the college campus, Reeda was a paragon of piety, known for her gentle nature and firm commitment to her faith.

In the vibrant world of college, Reeda stood out like a flower in full bloom. Her hazel eyes sparkled with wisdom, and a soft smile played on her lips. But what made her truly unique was the elegant hijab (headscarf worn by Muslim women) she wore – a magical scarf that wrapped her hair like a crown, shouting out her love for Allah.

This wasn't just any piece of cloth; it was a hijab, a superhero cape of modesty that Reeda wore with pride. The hijab wasn't just about fashion for her; it was a symbol of her commitment to Allah, like a little flag on a mountain saying, "I'm a Muslimah."

In the busy college halls, Reeda walked with confidence, and people couldn't help but notice. She wasn't flashy, but there was something about the way she carried herself that made others admire her. It wasn't just how she looked; it was who she was that left a mark on everyone.

Reeda was kind and humble, and everyone could feel it when she was around. She had a way of making people feel good with just a smile. It wasn't about being the loudest or the fanciest – it was about the way she treated others.

People liked and admired Reeda not just because she looked nice but because of the kind of person she was. She cared about others, she didn't give up easily when things got tough. Reeda wasn't just another face in the crowd; she was someone whose kindness and strength stood out in a busy college world.

As Reeda breezed through the college campus, her hijab swayed gently, adding a touch of mystery and grace. Some people were drawn to it like bees to honey, admiring her courage to stand out. But, of course, not everyone saw it that way. For some, her hijab was like a puzzle they couldn't figure out – weird and, unfortunately, sometimes even disgusting.

Being Reeda's roommate has been quite an adventure. When she first entered our college, she brought a gust of change with her. I vividly remember the day she engaged in a spirited debate about the Hijab on campus. The way she defended her beliefs and stood strong against those high-class women was nothing short of inspiring. The whole campus erupted in applause, and that moment marked the beginning of the legend of Reeda.

Her enthusiasm didn't stop there. Reeda used her blog as a platform to share her thoughts on Hijab, and her words resonated far beyond our college. The hashtag #Kashmiran became synonymous with her – a symbol of beauty with brains. It was incredible to witness her influence spreading not just across the country but globally.

However, as time passed, I noticed a change in Reeda. The powerhouse of energy and enthusiasm seemed to be fading. One day, she confided in me, "I'm missing my family terribly. I want to go back to Kashmir." Her eyes betrayed the strength she had displayed in the debate. It was a vulnerable moment.

In an effort to uplift her spirits, I decided to bring a piece of Kashmir to our room. I ordered her favourite Kashmiri dishes from Swiggy, hoping to evoke some nostalgia and comfort. As we sat together that night, sharing stories and relishing the flavours of home, I could see a flicker of the vibrant Reeda I had known.

That night, we decided to sleep in the same room. Sometimes, all you need is the warmth of companionship to alleviate the ache of homesickness. I felt grateful to be there for Reeda, just as she had been a pillar of strength to me too but who knew that was the last day I would be in touch with her?

Inspector Rajdeep's stern gaze bore into Jaspreet as he inquired, "Can you shed some light on what might have happened to her?"

Jaspreet, her expression a mix of concern and confusion, responded with a sigh, "Honestly, sir, I don't have a clue." The room buzzed with unanswered questions, creating an air of mystery that left Inspector Rajdeep grappling with the enigmatic circumstances surrounding Reeda. The suspense hung thick following the silence in the police station.

# DEAD BODY

# 17

In Reeda's hostel room, the unusual quietness alerted the warden, leading to concerns among residents. Reacting promptly, the warden called for security, and they assembled outside Room 203. The door was opened with an air of trepidation, revealing an unexpected sight - "Reeda was hanging from the ceiling fan, lifeless."

In the wake of the grim discovery, the shrill wails of sirens pierced the air as police vehicles hastily arrived at the scene. Uniformed officers, with stern expressions, swiftly cordoned off the area. Residents, bewildered and anxious, were ushered aside as the police commenced their investigation.

Officers methodically inspected the surroundings, jotting down notes and taking photographs. A sense of tension hung heavy, as a few residents were requested to accompany the police to the station for further questioning.

The usual rhythm of daily life had been replaced by the tense atmosphere of a continuing investigation, making the hostel's hallways feel burdened with an unsettling sense of uncertainty.

The unfolding events cast a spotlight on the interconnected lives within the hostel, each resident now a potential witness to the mysterious circumstances surrounding Reeda's demise. The investigation unfolded against the backdrop of this tight-knit community, shattering the illusion of tranquility that had once enveloped the hostel.

Inspector Rajdeep entered the hostel with an air of authority, his eyes scanning the surroundings as if seeking clues in every corner.

Inspector Rajdeep: (sternly) Warden, I need the facts. When was the last time someone saw her alive?

Hostel Warden: (nervously) Last night during dinner, sir. After that, no one noticed anything until the morning.

Inspector Rajdeep: (leaning in) Did anyone hear or see anything unusual during the night?

Security Officer: (looking perplexed) No, sir. It was quiet.

Inspector Rajdeep: (raising an eyebrow) Quiet? In a hostel filled with students? Let's not dance around it.

Were there any arguments, disputes, or anything out of the ordinary?

Hostel Warden: (hesitant) Well, there was a heated discussion about a week ago. Some students had differing opinions on a campus issue.

Inspector Rajdeep: (intrigued) A discussion? What was it about?

Security Officer: (nervously) It was about the upcoming cultural fest, sir. Some disagreements about the theme.

Inspector Rajdeep: (scrutinizing their reactions) Cultural fest disagreements leading to this? I find that hard to believe. There's more to this story, and I intend to find out. I want every detail, no matter how insignificant it seems.

Inspector Rajdeep: (sternly) And Warden, how did this happen under your watch?

Hostel Warden: (nervously) Sir, I assure you, we take the security of our residents seriously. This incident has left us all baffled.

Security Officer: (interjecting) We didn't notice anything unusual, sir. Everything seemed normal until now.

Inspector Rajdeep: (scrutinizing the surroundings) Did she show any signs of distress recently? Any unusual behavior?

Hostel Warden: (hesitant) Well, she did seem quieter than usual. But we thought it was the stress of exams.

Inspector Rajdeep: (leaning in) You need to keep a closer eye. Now, let's go over the events leading up to this tragedy. Every detail matters.

Security Officer: (nodding) Yes, sir. We'll cooperate fully with the investigation.

The inspector's questions echoed through the corridors, untangling the threads of the hostel's everyday life. The puzzle of Reeda's demise took shape, one question at a time.

## 9

Inspector Rajdeep, a seasoned investigator with a discerning gaze, was briskly passing through the college premises when a concerned student intercepted him. Acknowledging her presence, the inspector, donning a stern expression, nodded in agreement and motioned for her to share her information. Escorting her to the nearby police station, he anticipated that her revelations might hold the key to the perplexing case at hand.

In the dimly lit police station, the student hesitated for a moment before disclosing her observations about Reeda's peculiar behavior. She recounted witnessing Reeda spending time on the football field engaged in conversations with an unseen entity. The atmosphere in the station grew tense as the student detailed the eerie encounters she had witnessed, raising more questions about the circumstances leading to Reeda's tragic end.

Inspector Rajdeep listened intently as the student shared her observations, a furrow forming on his brow.

Inspector Rajdeep: (intrigued) So, she was talking to someone who wasn't there?

Student: (nodding) Yes, sir. Multiple times. I saw her on the football field, in her room, everywhere. It was like she had an imaginary friend.

Inspector Rajdeep: (thoughtful) Imaginary friend or something else? And the phone call?

Student: (hesitant) That was weird, sir. I overheard her shouting, but there was no one on the call. Just a wallpaper.

Inspector Rajdeep: (raising an eyebrow) Did you ever confront her about it?

Student: (shaking her head) No, sir. It felt odd, and I thought maybe she needed her space. But with all this happening, I thought I should tell someone.

Inspector Rajdeep: (serious) You did the right thing. This information might be crucial. Can you remember anything else? Anything she said or did that struck you as unusual?

Student: (pausing) Well, sir, she started praying regularly. Five times a day. That was surprising because she never used to do that before.

Inspector Rajdeep: (making notes) Praying, talking to an unseen companion, imaginary phone calls... this is getting interesting. Thank you for bringing this to my attention. It might help untie the mystery.

As the student left the police station, he delved deeper into the enigma surrounding Reeda's death. Inspector Rajdeep, now intrigued by the student's revelations, attentively absorbed the peculiarities of Reeda's actions. As the pieces of the jigsaw began to take shape, he realised that these seemingly unrelated details might be crucial in understanding the mystery surrounding Reeda's unusual behaviour and subsequent demise.

**One hour later…**

In the dimly lit police station, Inspector Rajdeep leaned over the cluttered desk, his gaze fixed on the case file. With a furrowed brow, he turned to his junior, seeking crucial details. "What about the postpartum details? We need to understand if there were any underlying issues," he inquired, his tone reflecting the urgency of the situation.

The junior, hunched over a stack of documents, responded, "Sir, we're expecting Reeda's postpartum report by Sunday. It's taking some time due to unforeseen circumstances, but we'll have it soon."

As the investigation pressed on, Inspector Rajdeep shifted his focus, "And her family? Are they on their way?" The junior hesitated briefly before replying, "Sir, there might be a delay. Some major reasons are hindering their immediate arrival."

Inspector Rajdeep then questioned "Did we find any suicide note in her room?"

The officer, flipping through the investigation notes, responded, "No, sir. There's no suicide note or any written explanation in her room." The absence of a suicide note added another layer of mystery to the case, leaving the investigators with more questions than answers.

Just as the gravity of the situation settled in the room, the junior added, "But, sir, we found something in Reeda's bag." He held up a small diary, its worn cover hinting at the potential secrets it might contain. The discovery of the diary added a layer of complexity to the investigation, setting the stage for a deeper exploration into Reeda's life and the mysterious circumstances surrounding her death.

# THE DIARY

# 18

*'Bilal, the man I thought would be my anchor, turned out to be a traitor, and his tragic end, found hanging from a tree in Baramullah, shattered the dreams we once shared.*

*On these pages, my feelings are poured out through the ink, holding the weight of my unspoken sadness. Betrayal has left scars on the trust I once cherished. As I explore my emotions, this diary becomes a quiet friend, soaking in the honesty of my feelings. The ache of losing and the harsh reality of deception are woven into a story told in the language of a broken heart.*

*Every word serves as an outlet, expressing the deep sorrow and the shattered dreams of a future that can never be.'*

***– From Reeda's Journal***

9

As Inspector Rajdeep meticulously flips through Reeda's diary, searching for clues within the intimate pages, his gaze pauses on a particular entry. There, amidst the handwritten emotions, he discovers a page that seems to hold an unusual revelation. Reeda's upsetting words unfold a narrative that could potentially shed light on the tangled web of her emotions. The diary, now a key piece in the investigation, becomes a portal into the depths of Reeda's soul, offering glimpses into the enigmatic circumstances surrounding her life and, perhaps, the events leading to her tragic end.

The page read :

Today as I woke up, Jaspreet had left me a note on the table saying :

Hey Reeda,

*I hope you find this note as soon as you wake up. I had to leave for Jalandhar early in the morning due to a family emergency – my cousin's funeral. I didn't want to disturb your sleep since you seemed tired from yesterday.*

*I promise to come back very soon. Meanwhile, take care of yourself, and if you need anything, don't hesitate to reach out. You're strong, and I know you'll manage well.*

See you soon,

**Jaspreet**

"Jaspreet is like Geet from "Jab We Met" – talkative, bubbly, and always ready for an adventure. Her life's mantra? "Main apni favorite hoon!" And just like Piku, she manages to bring a sense of humor even in the most mundane situations. You know what she says when things get tough? "Babu mushay, zindagi badi honi chahiye, lambi nahi!" Jaspreet, with her Bollywood charm, turns every ordinary day into a blockbuster.

I will miss her!"

Inspector Rajdeep, least interested on this topic, turns the page pointing his eyes straight on the black marked alphabets written in cursive writing all over the diary.

Another page read:

College life was like a rollercoaster, filled with ups and downs. When I first landed there, everything was a bit overwhelming. But hey, then came Jaspreet, Ayan, and Sarah – my squad. We laughed, we goofed around, and suddenly, things started making sense.

And then, there was this day on the football field. Moosa, this dude with a knack for making the perfect passes, entered the scene. One stray ball brought us together. We started with the usual sports banter, but as the conversation flowed, we discovered shared interests and different viewpoints. Who knew that a game of football could kickstart a whole new chapter in my college saga? Life's full of surprises, nah?

Okay, well! Let me elaborate on the day!

In Aligarh University, Moosa and I met during his football match, and that moment sparked a special connection between us. After the game, Moosa approached and we began our journey together.

One day in the university park, Moosa opened up about his feelings, saying he knew there was something special between us since our first eye contact on the football field. He asked, "Will you be mine?" Under the shade of trees, I agreed, sealing our commitment.

As our story progressed, Moosa showed his love in various ways. Climbing up to my hostel room, he expressed his feelings intimately, creating a special space for our connection. Though the details of our private moments are personal, they were filled with love and understanding.

Moosa continued to express his affection by kissing my forehead whenever we met on campus. During my fever, he took care of me, showing a caring side that deepened our bond. Our romantic moments included restaurant dates, turning ordinary times into memorable experiences.

In addition to these planned gestures, Moosa's secret visits to my hostel room added an element of surprise to our relationship. In the quiet of the night, he would sneak in, creating a special moment for us.

Moosa, the daredevil! This guy would climb up to my hostel window like a real-life Bahubali. Nights turned into our own little adventures, filled with laughter, talks, and maybe a bit of mischief. His bold moves and sense of humour made him the Bahubali of our little escapades. Life at the hostel got a lot more entertaining with Moosa's unexpected entries and his knack for turning ordinary nights into memorable ones.

Moosa, that guy, was like a magician on speed dial. Blink, and there he was, handing me stuff like he had a direct line to Hogwarts or something. It was strange, but in a cool, mysterious way. The delivery speed? Impressive. The how-did-he-do-that factor? Mind-boggling. College got a bit more interesting with Moosa and his magical deliveries, I'll give him that.

It was like having a magical friend who could conjure up whatever you wished for. From snacks to surprise gifts, Moosa made every day feel like a spontaneous celebration. His mysterious deliveries and charming personality added a touch of magic to our otherwise routine college life.

One day, Moosa brought me a teddy bear, and I was really happy until one day emails started popping up on my screen. That's when I realized that Moosa was writing to me: 'Hey, little hon! Remember the teddy I brought you? Uff! It meant a great deal to me. I waited for so many days, but every day, I saw you from the hidden camera placed on the eye of the laptop. I observed you studying or doing some other work until yesterday when I saw you undressing in front of the teddy bear. What a scene it was! Thank you so much for providing me with content that I can now post on different sites and earn money. Haha! You were of great use, man.

I shared everything with Moosa about the disaster on my wedding day and how Rayan took advantage of me. He started reminding me of all that and blamed me for my existence along with blackmailing me. I had no one to share this with and I couldn't reach out to my family as well.

I started calling him and he constantly asked me to die because I didn't deserve this life. Now I think he is right, I really don't deserve this anymore. I am quitting without an official suicide note, but the emails on my laptop and the phone call logs, along with my pictures with him on my mobile, are still there. To whomever it may concern, please ensure he is held accountable after I leave this world. He betrayed me. Every man betrays me in this world, except for my dad and brothers. I am weary of everything. I am becoming a burden to my family by acting like a depressed creature.

**– From Reeda's Journal**

## 9

In a swift moment, Inspector Rajdeep's eyes widened as he read the troubling entry from Reeda's diary. He swiftly grabbed his phone and barked orders to his team, demanding the immediate retrieval of the victim's laptop, mobile, and any crucial evidence.

With a sense of urgency, the investigative team combed through Reeda's belongings, carefully scrutinizing each item for any hint that could shed light on the mysterious circumstances. Despite their diligent efforts, no concrete evidence emerged.

Inspector Rajdeep (frustrated): We need to find a clue, anything that connects the dots!

Officer (on the phone): Sir, we've checked, but there's nothing significant. It's like she erased her digital footprint.

Inspector Rajdeep (grumbling): Dammit! We're missing something. (pauses) Call the principal, now! We need details on this Moosa guy. He's connected to her, and I want to know how.

Realizing the need for external collaboration, Inspector Rajdeep decided to delve deeper into Reeda's connections, particularly focusing on Moosa, a football champion in the college. The urgency in his voice as he called the school principal hinted at the gravity of the situation, and an undercover air of suspense wrapped the unreleased investigation.

The principal, caught off guard by the late-night call, promised to provide all the necessary details of Moosa by the next morning. The tension stayed fit as the promise hung in the air, leaving Inspector Rajdeep wrestling with the conundrum that was Reeda's tragic story.

**The next morning: -**

Inspector Rajdeep (perplexed): What do you mean, no Moosa? Are you sure?

Principal (assertive): I've double-checked, Inspector. There's no record of any student named Moosa in the past five years. And we don't have a football champion by that name.

Inspector Rajdeep (thoughtful): This is getting stranger by the minute. Okay, thank you. I need to dig deeper into this.

The revelation added another layer of mystery, leaving Inspector Rajdeep with more questions than answers.

# OPEN AND SHUT CASE

# 19

Inspector Rajdeep sighed, staring at the cluttered evidence on his desk. The mysterious case of Reeda's death had taken an unexpected turn. He decided to reach out to his childhood friend, Nisha, a clinical psychologist and graphologist, seeking her expertise.

With a sense of urgency, Rajdeep dialed Nisha's number.

Inspector Rajdeep: Nisha, I need your help. There's a peculiar case, and I'm hitting dead ends. It involves a girl named Reeda who, according to a witness, seemed to talk to an invisible person.

Nisha, always intrigued by challenging cases, responded promptly.

Nisha: Go on.

Inspector Rajdeep explained the findings so far – the distressing diary, the mysterious figure named Moosa, and the witness account of Reeda talking to an invisible person.

Nisha: I'll be there soon, Rajdeep. Let me analyze the handwriting and provide some psychological insights. We might get a clearer picture of what Reeda was going through.

Rajdeep felt a glimmer of hope as he awaited Nisha's expertise to untangle the complexities of Reeda's situation. The collaboration between law enforcement and psychology was about to shed light on the shadows of a mysterious tragedy.

Meanwhile, Reeda's father, and her brothers, Abrar, Rahi, Razaq and Umer, entered the police station with a heavy heart. Inspector Rajdeep, sensing the gravity of the situation, approached them.

Inspector Rajdeep: (with empathy) Mr. Reshi, I understand this is a difficult time for your family. We are doing everything in our power to uncover the truth behind Reeda's passing.

Rahi, with a mix of sadness and frustration, responded.

Rahi: Inspector, we never imagined our sister's life would take such a turn. What happened to her, and why?

Inspector Rajdeep: We're investigating every angle, Mr. Reshi. I assure you, we won't rest until we find the answers. Please, have a seat.

As they sat down, Abrar couldn't contain his emotions.

Abrar: (with teary eyes) Inspector, Reeda was the soul of our family. We need to know what drove her to this point.

Inspector Rajdeep: (compassionately) I understand your concerns. We're looking into every aspect of her life. If you could provide any information that might help, it would be invaluable.

Umer, the youngest brother, couldn't hold back his tears.

Umer: (choked up) She was always there for us, Inspector. How did everything fall apart?

Inspector Rajdeep: (softly) We're trying to piece together the puzzle. Your cooperation is crucial. We will get to the bottom of this.

The room echoed with the weight of unspoken grief as the investigation unfolded, and Reeda's family grappled with the sudden and tragic loss.

## 9

**Another scene, same hour:**

Nisha, the clinical psychologist, entered the police station with a calm demeanor. Inspector Rajdeep, recognizing her, approached her.

Inspector Rajdeep: Nisha, thank you for coming. We're dealing with a complex case here.

Nisha: (nodding) I've heard. Tell me everything you know, and I'll do my best to provide insights.

Inspector Rajdeep briefed Nisha on the mysterious circumstances surrounding Reeda's death, mentioning the invisible person and the unusual diary entries.

Nisha: (thoughtfully) Let me see the diary first. Hand me any other relevant evidence you have.

Inspector Rajdeep handed over the diary and shared information about the emails from Moosa and Reeda's emotional struggles.

Nisha: (flipping through the diary) It seems Reeda was grappling with deep emotional pain. I'll analyze this further. Now, about Moosa, I suggest we investigate that angle thoroughly.

Inspector Rajdeep agreed, and they discussed a plan to trace Moosa and gather more information.

Nisha: (with determination) We need to understand the psychological aspects of Reeda's life. I'll work on a profile to shed light on her mental state.

Inspector Rajdeep thanked Nisha for her assistance, recognizing that her expertise would be crucial in solving the complexities of the case.

Nisha meticulously examined Reeda's history, considering every detail provided by her family. After thorough research, she approached Inspector Rajdeep with a revelation.

Nisha: (thoughtfully) Inspector, it appears that Reeda was experiencing hallucinations. There is no record of Moosa in her life; he seems to be a creation of her imagination.

Inspector Rajdeep: (puzzled) Hallucinations? Why would she imagine someone like Moosa?

Nisha: (explaining) Reeda went through a traumatic event – the betrayal by Rayan, death of Bilal and the subsequent emotional distress. Hallucinations often manifest as a coping mechanism, especially during times of extreme stress. In her case, Moosa became a figure she could confide in, someone who provided comfort during her moments of vulnerability.

Inspector Rajdeep: (realizing) So, Moosa was a product of her mind to cope with her pain?

Nisha: (nodding) Exactly. Her mind created a companion, a support system that didn't exist in reality. It's not uncommon for individuals facing intense emotional disturbance to develop such coping mechanisms.

Note:- Nisha, delving deeper into Reeda's psyche, discovered a significant piece of evidence on her blog. She presented a blog post where Reeda had poured out her feelings and emotions, unknowingly giving insight into the roots of her hallucination.

Nisha: (sharing the blog post) This blog post reveals Reeda's inner struggles. In her writing, she vividly describes her pain and the need for someone to understand her. It's here that Moosa first appears, a character born from the depths of her despair.

Inspector Rajdeep examined the blog post, recognizing the connection between Reeda's traumatic past and the emergence of Moosa in her life.

Inspector Rajdeep: (contemplating) So, Moosa was a creation of her need for support, a manifestation of her desire for companionship during difficult times.

Nisha: (affirming) Yes, exactly. Her writing serves as a window into her subconscious, showing us the origins of this hallucination.

Armed with this newfound understanding, Inspector Rajdeep and Nisha continued to piece together the intricate puzzle of Reeda's mental state, seeking a clearer picture of the events that led to her tragic demise. Inspector Rajdeep, absorbed in the mystery, received SI Gautam, who brought with him the postmortem report. The room held a tense atmosphere as they began to examine the details.

SI Gautam: (handing over the report) The postmortem report confirms it as a suicide case. No signs of foul play were found.

Inspector Rajdeep: (examining the report) Any specific findings that could shed light on her mental state?

SI Gautam: (nodding) The autopsy indicates no external injuries. However, traces of medication used to treat anxiety and depression were found in her system.

Inspector Rajdeep: (pondering) So, she was battling mental health issues.

SI Gautam: (confirming) Yes, it seems like a case of deep emotional distress.

Nisha: See, I told you. It's an open and shut case.

Inspector Rajdeep: Unbelievable!

9

**Twenty minutes later: -**

Inspector Rajdeep and Nisha sat down with Reeda's family in the small, dimly lit room of the police station. Mr. Reshi, Rahi, Abrar and Umer anxiously awaited any news about Reeda. The air was heavy with the weight of unspoken fears.

Rajdeep: (with a composed yet empathetic tone) We have been investigating Reeda's case thoroughly, and we've found some crucial information that needs to be shared.

Nisha: (calmly) Reeda was facing severe mental distress. The so-called Moosa she mentioned—there is no record of such a person. It appears she was experiencing hallucinations.

Mrs. Reshi: (eyes widening in disbelief) Hallucinations? But she seemed so normal!

Rajdeep: (nodding) Mental health struggles often go unnoticed. Reeda was adept at concealing her pain, but the signs were there.

Nisha: (explaining) We found evidence in her blog, where she wrote about Moosa and the events she believed were happening. It was a manifestation of her inner struggles.

Umer: (voice breaking) But why? Why didn't she tell us?

Rajdeep: (gentle) Sometimes, individuals facing mental health issues find it challenging to open up. They fear judgment or burdening their loved ones.

Nisha: (compassionate) It's crucial to be aware of the signs and support those who may be silently battling their own minds.

Abrar, the dearest brother to Reeda got numb and went mute.

**The room fell into a heavy silence as the gravity of Reeda's silent struggle sank in.**

# RAZAQ

# 20

Assalamualaikum everyone, I'm Razaq, Reeda's brother. I don't talk much. Neither have you seen me highlighted in the chapters before much.

I am here to share few words about my sister.

We didn't share the closest bond, and I carried some resentment because it felt like she got more attention from our family. Now, as I write this, I realize how much I miss her.

Reeda, or 'Kashmiran,' as many knew her, was more than just my sister; she was a strong soul dealing with hidden emotions. Today, I'm here on her website, not to fix things or say sorry, but to remember her. These posts hold her thoughts and feelings, telling the story of 'Kashmiran.' I want to honor her, recognizing the struggles she faced that we might not have fully understood. Each poem and post is a reminder of her unique view of life.

This isn't about regret or what we could have done differently. It's about appreciating the pieces of her she shared online. This tribute is my way of keeping 'Kashmiran's' spirit alive.

Reeda's struggles with mental health weren't obvious, concealed behind her beautiful words. I share this not to dwell on past grievances but to emphasize the importance of mental well-being. We often overlook the silent battles people face, not realizing the impact of their unspoken pain.

Her unexpected departure reminds us that those closest to us may carry unseen burdens. Let's create an environment where discussing mental health is encouraged and embraced. Reeda's legacy goes beyond her stories; it's a call for compassion, understanding, and a commitment to destigmatize mental health. Let this post be a source of comfort and encouragement, urging everyone to reach out, listen, and comprehend the unspoken battles others might be facing. In honoring her memory, let us strengthen the importance of empathy, compassion, and open conversations about mental health. May her legacy inspire a greater awareness that could potentially make a difference in someone else's life.

Ameen'!

# THE FUNERAL

# 21

The funeral day dawned with heavy hearts as family and relatives gathered to bid a final farewell to Reeda.

Rahi, a man of strong conviction, spoke to a group of mourners. "In the face of loss, we turn to our faith for solace. Islam teaches us that every soul shall taste death, and today, our dear Reeda has embarked on her final journey. May Allah grant her peace."

He then addressed the mourners, "Inna lillahi wa inna ilayhi raji'un. Today, we bid farewell to our beloved Reeda. Let us remember her in our prayers and seek Allah's mercy for her soul."

One of Reeda's maternal uncles with a heavy heart, added, "May Allah grant Reeda the highest place in Jannah. Let us come together in prayer and support for the family during this difficult period."

In accordance with Islamic traditions, Reeda's four brothers took charge of the funeral procedures. They gently placed her body on a simple bier and carried it to the designated burial ground.

Amidst silent prayers and Quranic verses, they lowered her body into the grave, ensuring it faced the qiblah. Each brother took turns placing soil into the grave, symbolising the return to the earth.

Abrar, deeply affected, spoke softly, "Inna lillahi wa inna ilayhi raji'un. From Allah we come, and to Him, we return."

Mohsin chacha, a pillar of support, asked everyone to send prayers to their beloved child who committed a sin when her mental state was not stable.

As they lowered Reeda into her final resting place, a collective silence enveloped the scene, broken only by the sobs of those who held her dear.

As the brothers completed the burial, they sought forgiveness for any shortcomings and offered supplications for Reeda's soul. The gathering then dispersed, leaving behind a quiet burial site that would, with time, become a place of remembrance and prayer for those who loved 'Kashmiran.'

As the Reshi brothers returned home after the burial, their mother, Mrs. Reshi, awaited them with a heavy heart. The atmosphere was mournful, and the weight of grief hung in the air. Rahi, the eldest brother, approached his mother, who sat in a corner.

Rahi: (softly) "Ammi, we've laid Reeda to rest with the respect she deserved."

Mrs. Reshi: (bursting out in tears) "My daughter... My Reeda. *Yie keth peth gow* (How could this happen?"

Abrar, Umer, and Razaq gathered around, each expressing their own silent sorrow. Mrs. Reshi held a framed picture of Reeda, tracing the contours of her face with a trembling hand.

Abrar: "Ammi, we need to stay strong for each other. Reeda would want that."

Mrs. Reshi: (choked up) "I never thought I'd see the day when I bury my own child. *'Su oas moun jiger'..*" (She was my heart)

Umer: "Ammi, we're here for you. We'll get through this together."

***In the quiet room, everyone could hear the sadness in the soft cries of a family dealing with an incredibly hard loss.***

# PIECE OF FINE ART!

The one who stole my heart,
Was a piece of fine art.
His appearance outlining the brushed hair and black shirt,
Enlightened my inner self to have a fresh start.
The eyes hypnotising, with those delighted looks,
All he did was to rent a place in my good books.
The first view of his lips, his nose, his hair,
Structured the gem which is very rare.
By connecting our souls, he fed me with a surprise,
I hold him in my heart today as a sumptuous prize.
Now, his presence by my side,
Is enough for me to explore worldwide.
Barely had I thought, he would end up being mine,
Yes he is definitely the one, with whom I can rise and shine.

– The poem Reeda wrote on Moosa

**R.I.P**

# EPILOGUE

Much like Reeda, each one of us inhabit a place that gives us warmth, comfort and a fierce unconditional protection against all the hurt and pain directed at us. That place is our home, our safe abode during storms and our strongest defense against adversities.

Much like Reeda, that home often gets destroyed. Suffering from excruciating blows repeatedly, unfed for too long and yet exploiting the last dregs of its resources to combat with the formidable challenges thrown repeatedly at it, at one point it breaks down.

Yet, it has to stand up again on its wobbling, wasted feet to carry the load of our being within it; because no matter what it cannot abandon us, it does not choose to, at least. Such in-built, inherent and absolute is that beautiful, bountiful, diversified habitat of ours.

Commonly, we call it- the Mind. That precious, motherly, protective Mind of human beings.

We go through the fire like the iron to be smelted into shape and even as we are washed by acid rain, we are still expected to stand strong not just bearing the pain but also act like nothing burnt in the first place. Well, some of us do succeed in doing so while others fade away in the fight. But all of that is done by who? Who is to be credited for all the struggles we encountered head on, all the battles we fought-losing some and winning others? Who houses all regrets we might still be harboring deep inside, parched of happiness, love and warmth? It is our mind.

Unlike Reeda, our mind may not always turn its protective mode on so fiercely that it teleports us to a place where we can be happy and safe even if it is just an illusion, even if it is just momentary- and yet, crash down just as fiercely one day. But it may end up doing so. When it does, the report might simply put, 'Death by suicide while battling with Schizophrenia'. Is it truly fair to judge the entire matter so simply and dismissively?

Our Mind employs every ounce of its energy, providing every inch of its place to accommodate us and our lives. Why not treat it with love and care? Why not dedicate equal gentleness to it, the way we treat our body? Why associate shame, doubt and weakness when the mind requires help; but pity, sympathy and support when the body needs it?

Let us first be kind to ourselves and recognize the power and prowess of the mind- what it does and can potentially do for us, where it may go wrong, how it can be supported and most importantly, how it can be taken care of. Let us pledge to take care of our Safe Haven- our Mind just as much as it takes care of us.

And next time a Reeda shows up in the news, could that sigh be slightly heavier with generous sympathy and most importantly, respect? It was just another soldier returning home defeated from the battle of life. Maybe one more hand on her hands, one more smile to face her way, one more shoulder to cry on could have provided her with the extra ammunition required to win this battle.

We always know when the mind craves some comfort, a space to scream freely, then reach a place of solace in our life. The only barrier is reaching out. Maybe we can convince each other that all of us are made of a soft flesh which needs some tenderness. And we all can reach out for help as it is also waiting right there on the other side of the door.

That, it is not too hard to come together and say,

*"But, know that it was a thorny path with enemies everywhere*

*I hope you never forget the one who throw flowers on the road for you When you're laughing, don't forget the one who cries*

*Cause they live a day on your smile"*

- *Snooze, Agust D ft Ryuichi Sakamoto, WOOSUNG*

*[ Translation from Genius lyrics ]*

**ARPITA MAJI**
**Consultant and Consultant psychologist**
**Guest Faculty, IMS, MAKAUT**

# NOTE TO READERS

Hello Readers,

As someone working in the field of clinical psychology, especially as a clinical intern, I've realized the importance of connecting with people on a deeper level. Instead of writing poems, which not everyone enjoys, I've decided to share an important message through a novel.

I'm not sure how well it will be understood, but I hope it sparks some understanding and curiosity in the minds of those who read it, without any reservations.

Life's like a puzzle, and mental health is a piece that can't be ignored. It's like having a good friend who needs a little extra care.

Just like we know how to put a band-aid on a cut, we can also give mental health first aid. Pay attention when your friends or family seem a bit off, and don't be afraid to ask how they're doing.

A listening ear, a kind word, and suggesting they talk to someone professional—these are our mental health first aid tools. Small acts of kindness can be big help.

Let's make looking out for each other's mental health a thing we all do. We're like a team, supporting each other through the ups and downs.

Take care and stay kind,

– Soudia Parveen

# MORE BOOKS BY SOUDIA PARVEEN

Soudia
Parveen

Books are available at Amazon, Flipkart, Kindle Worldwide.

www.ingramcontent.com/pod-product-compliance
Lightning Source LLC
LaVergne TN
LVHW012058160826
845678LV00014B/2865

* 9 7 8 9 3 5 6 7 3 7 0 0 6 *